DUNES REVIEW

COVER IMAGE :
"Off the Path" by Ann Willey
Image courtesy of the artist.

*In loving memory of Roland B. Ninomiya
and others we have lost*

DUNES REVIEW

VOLUME 27 ISSUE 1

JULY 2023

CONTENTS

Land Acknowledgement

Dunes Review is published on the traditional lands of the Grand Traverse Band of Ottawa and Chippewa Indians. It is important to understand the long-standing history that has brought us to reside on the land, and to seek to understand our place within that history. We thank the Anishinaabe people for allowing us to be here today.

Cover Artist's Statement

I grew up on the shores of Lake Michigan in a large family of artists, writers, and musicians. In college I studied printmaking and worked many years as a graphic artist and illustrator. Painting is now the main focus of my art practice.

I maintain an art studio in the woods by a little creek, gathering inspiration from the wildlife around me. In my paintings I find myself exploring the realms of family life, dreams, myths and memories. Some of the reoccurring themes in my work are nurturing, impermanence, spiritual journeys and growth, and our connection to nature and each other. Influenced by a love of folk art and magical realism, my paintings have a narrative quality, as if the scene is part of a story or a dream. The objects, animals and figures have the potential to represent more than just themselves, and could at any moment transform. I am trying to glimpse a world where everything is sentient, where connections are made and nature infuses our humanity. I hope all of this combines to create a psychological dimension beneath the surface of the imagery, and to reflect the complexity of the many worlds we all share.

Over my career, I have worked in many media, including fiber arts. My series of prints and cards are created from my original work using acrylics, gouache, and pastels. I have shown my work in many exhibitions and galleries over the years. My paintings can be found at Higher Art Gallery in Traverse City, and on my website at annwilley.com.

—Ann Willey

Editors' Notes

While we were at work preparing this issue, a dear friend of nearly forty years ended his life. I learned too late the depth of his struggles with depression. We who loved him are heartbroken — heartbroken to lose him, and heartbroken to think that we could not do more to ease his suffering.

When Andrew Stevens's essay came to us, we felt it was important to share his voice, with supportive material, to shine some light on the experiences of people who suffer from depression and suicidal ideation. We describe how we put together this special section later on in this volume. But here I want to say that suddenly I was aware of the issue of suicide and saw it everywhere. And I saw how we do not often speak about this, or speak about it completely.

Friends in the helping professions tell me that the question it is imperative to ask, "Are you thinking about harming yourself?" is the one we are least likely to ask. It feels too direct, too intrusive. Yet it is the way to open up a conversation about these feelings and fears. We hope you find some thought-provoking and helpful voices in this journal. We hope you pass it around. We hope you find words to speak with the ones you love.

— *Teresa Scollon*

All the new thinking is about loss, says Robert Hass in "Meditation at Lagunitas," one of my favorites. *In this it resembles all the old thinking.* And it's true, not just in our thinking but in our realities: loss is all around, always lurking, and in some seasons, it seems, not merely seeping in at the baseboards but relentless, pressing in from all sides. In this issue, as in so many we curate, the theme of loss pulses steadily. Sometimes it comes with a flip side, a redemption, a culminating comfort. But just as often, it doesn't. It just hurts. We mourn, and we don't know what comes next. Other times, it's the threat of loss instead: what if this ends? What if everything is about to change? What if nothing ever does?

Beauty in the face of grief, grief in the face of beauty; two sides of that old stubborn coin always riding around in our pockets. "Sometimes it's too much," like Onna Solomon writes, "…the blooming and dying in predictable succession." Yes, it's too much, and yet we still sit with it all. We carry it, and we press on.

— *Jennifer Yeatts*

Stephanie Keep
ON EARTH, AS IT IS

I grow drunk off it:
spring scent river bloom.

We go walking on the loamy gravel
in my heaven.

Sunshine or snow
we ride high on the momentum
of seasons.

I have been taken by the river.
Runoff in my bones, my veins.
Runoff my middle name.

> Count my wealth in rivers
> and hours spent traipsing it.

We are at that point of transformation.
I wear my winter sleeves rolled up.

We think it is in winter
but in spring we are tested.
We speak of *hardiness*,
enduring in the same breath as
viable and *new growth*.

I hear a rustling start
and watch for the wind
                downstream.

I bend to inspect a shoot along the trail
and straighten in the rain
to look at the sun.

Michael Mark
IN THE MARINE LAYER

They look like they slept here,
         in the open. Or, despite the signs,
in *Unstable Caves*.

They orbit each other. They lost
         something –
something

         they want back badly –
maybe last night. I have stopped
         my morning walk

to watch, half
         disguised on the cloud-curtain's
other side. Something about them

         belongs here,

with the tossed-up kelp, crabs
         rolled on their backs, bellies
gutted by gulls.

The two keep circling,
         searching. And even in this haze,
maybe because of it, maybe

because I am in it
         with them, it's clear – their slumps,
stringy hair, almost transparent

clothes which appear
         to be their only – something
forever is happening. I brave another step.

The fog takes them

         from me, I feel.

Patricia Aya Williams
OMEN

a crow flew in
through the open

door
of our kitchen

upsetting the dog
and teatime

banging itself
hard

on the window
desperate

for a way
out

you cursed
as it shuddered

back to sky
a single

dark feather
falling

in its wake
I grieve

for what is
lost between us

what is
to come

Rana Tahir
SOLDIERS IN SHOWBIZ
pronounced "show-beez"

Along al Balajat where the gulf comes,
a moment staring at their surrounding
left them stranded in a firebombed
pizza palace, with arcade games
and animatronic bears. There years
later, malfunctioning or starting
suddenly, a kiddie coaster shaped
as a caterpillar traveling fast
without seatbelts through an apple
made of metal frames and golden
string lights. On one side, my parents,
on the other, the open sea.

Pablo Piñero Stillmann
WEATHER REPORT

It's not cold here, love. Not even
close to how it was in our city.
It snowed hard—remember?—
that time we met for hot chocolate &
innocent conversation. Why did I blurt
out a story about my grandfather's frostbite
in the '42 war? It's not cold here, love.
Not like when you grabbed my jacket
to keep from slipping on ice. It burns,
how we both left in the stupid summer,
each to a different place sans freezing
winters. Why? Everything belonged
to us. You were sick of the snow & I
wanted to burrow in it forever. All
my winter clothes are now hibernating
or dead, can't tell, in an extra-large white
garbage bag above my closet. Nights
when I yearn for the sorrow, I sleep
on the bag pretending it's mid-
February powder. Or I place all garments
on the faux wood floor & make angels.
Then I burn the clothes, camper's
mug of brandy at my chest. In the morning
the bag reappears, whole again, yours
again, above my closet. These bones are
lukewarm & hollow. The mind is pelted
with sleet. My trunk grew crooked
for reasons certain & not. Only what
shouldn't is going cold. Without
you the goddamn sun shines eternal.

Rado Rochallyi
VECTOR AND TERMINATION

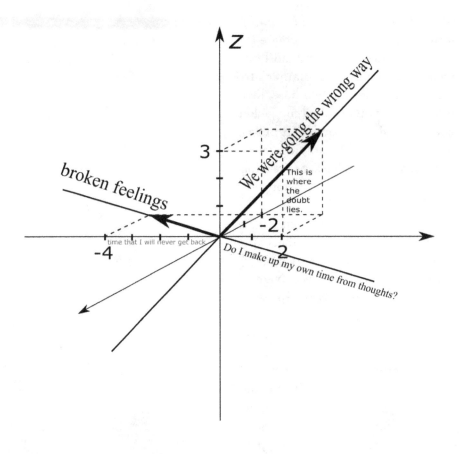

Ellen Lord
NORTH COUNTRY ELEGY
after Jim Harrison

I love these raw winter nights,
a thousand critters you can't see
hibernate under a shroud of snow.
My memory takes me back to another life,
how we would skate a northern lake,
warmed by desire.
I was oblivious then to the mercy
solitude could bestow.
My body has been betraying me
for a long time now —
I'm not quite sure anymore
how I learned to be alone.

Onna Solomon
FIRST SNOW IN NOVEMBER

We didn't get all the leaves up
and now there they lie and there
they will remain. This week I will
celebrate cousin Molly's coming birth
(note to self: dig up that small
blue sweater and hand it down)
and a decade of my first son's life —
bake a cake and endure
three hours of a trampoline park/arcade
then send texts of thanks
for Mario Cart and Fifa World Cup
for the Switch (shout out
to those who know what that sentence means!) —
and before all that, I will make
a page to raise funds for my friend
whose cancer is back. Earlier
in the month, our plantings from
last year died gloriously —
the honeysuckle a shock
of red and orange slim leaves
flaming in the breeze, lumbago blooming
their last blue, the long grasses
a fragrant pallid frenzy.

Sometimes it's too much, the ordinary
richness of this liminal month,
the blooming and dying
in predictable succession. Now our car's
covered in snow because the garage
is still cluttered with summer's detritus —
boogie boards, potting soil, ball bins
and bikes, the soccer net tangled
around the mower. We didn't get to it.
We never get to all of it. Instead, we walk
a mile to Argus Farm Stop in the cold

gray, just to be together and breathe the changing
air—the four of us marching along
with the near distant sound of the crowd cheering
in the Big House. We won,
but I don't care.

Ellen White Rook
D-R-U-S-E-N

When I look through one eye, everything is hero-clear, brilliant and discrete, a stunning and precise universe. Through the other, the world has the look of dying afternoon. At the edges, object fritter: yellow film smears storefront windows, each mountain view, a cut-rate reproduction.

At my request, the ophthalmologist spells out loud: D-U-S-E-N. A search discovers super geometric collaboration with psychology in mind, a fictional detective, the litigator who focuses on covenants not to compete. Nothing I see connects with the tiny spots my doctor found.

She missed the R.

D-R-U-S-E-N comes from German, for geode—spheres sparkling with glittering omissions.

Scotopic vision. My future clawing at the present moment's illusion of clarity.

It's the center that my eyes won't hold. Soon, some things will spring from nowhere, others, disappear. Miracles of cardinals and oak trees, nightmares of vehicles and pedestrians.

Today, my eyes work as wings adapting to unbalanced strength and wind. I fly into this dispersed dimension which comes from that dead brilliance, plush-deep and beautiful, the darkest blue, a sky fallen out of clouds.

Onna Solomon
WINTER IN EBERWHITE WOODS

Pond frozen over—the one
where the turtles bask
in other seasons

doused in sunlight
through the bare trees.
See, I say—the green scum

encased below inches of ice.
Frogs, one son claims, are sleeping
down there. There's still

moss on the logs, the other notes as
with all his force he yanks
on the tree limb stuck

in ice. It does not budge. This morning
I listened to the recorded voice
of an old poet saying, *In every joy:*

sadness. In every sadness:
joy. Waiting to be dislodged, softened,
so the fragrance of it—growth

or decay—can be released.
My sons slip past
in their sturdy boots

wrestle each other down
to the hard surface, now in tears,
now in fits of laughter.

Mad Howard
UME

Plums bloom in the latest winter,
When the rains come and the leaves

Decompose to golden sludge;
The flowers pink

In their newness. The snow is
still crunching under boots.

Fingers pick the
Petals and search

For the spice of something.
It is a bright salvation

a frozen drink of mist.

January Pearson
ODE TO ORANGE TREES

No rain
and no rain, yet
your heat-tolerant talent
to dream up juice.
For your shade,
so generously offered,
an umbrella to scorched
skin. Leaves
green as chameleons,
rarely turning color,
persistent through winter's
longest days.
Papery white blossoms,
suds overflowing,
toughening into dimpled
thick skin. That your tiny
flowers can transform
into a summer staple.
For your strength,
your branches carrying
pounds of fruit
to their fullness.
For the luck of plucking
from a friend's tree
one that hasn't traveled
miles in semi-trucks
through hot traffic.
For your kindness
in letting us take from you,
and take from you.
For your honey
beneath the bitter.

Russell Thorburn
HONEY DRINKERS

If you don't believe in slow motion
there's no reason for you to listen
to the fingerprints of their flutter,
or watch their bills collect honey
from the feeder as if the world
were standing still. They leave
it exactly where it was when
they hum somewhere else,
you disbelieving you have seen
them at all, as you watch your wife
close the balcony door. Inside, her bra
is unaccounted for and her nude
body becomes this way to picture
heaven as she looks for her clothes.
A fleeting, ephemeral moment,
as you are left hanging in air
like a honey drinker in the drizzle
that morning decides to sprinkle
upon you shirtless and humming.

Ellen Lord
ANGLER

How my body arched —
arched, his lure finding
its way in silky shadow
to pierce my lips,
his filament taut and urgent
— and I rose, rose

in the thunderous cascade
of a surging waterfall
a quiver
of salmon colored dazzle
glorious in the mist.

Paul Maxbauer
FOR DENNIS, IN MEMORIAM

In the late afternoon we walked down a narrow footpath
to the river through a thick stand of willows,
aware that the valley we entered was frequented
by grizzly bears, one being spotted the day before.

We waded a long curving arc of the river,
observed small mayflies hatching, tiny gray sailboats
on the water, trout rising to them, and swallows
working the airspace above. We happily caught

and released many beautiful Yellowstone cutthroats.
Both of us, it seemed, moved and casted in a dream-like trance,
so that we were surprised by a strong thunderstorm
blowing in over the mountains. We pulled on our raincoats,

hunkered down on a gravel bar amid the wind and pouring rain,
like monks at prayer, hoods drawn tight, Dennis with a stub of cigar
between his teeth, still glowing. Then the rain let up, the storm passed,
and as dusk turned to night, the trout began to rise again.

Kurt Olsson
CATCH

Without knowing you practice beauty.
The behind the back. Hard juke and feint ankle-
rolling your shadow. The sweet level swing
of hickory winched deep inside the bone.
You practice beauty with what's at hand.
Wiffleballs, friction tape, Nerf footballs,
wadded socks, Frisbees and apple cores,
spittle-slick tennis balls, homework papers
peppered red with demerits, wingnuts.
Out back, practicing the over the shoulder,
you are immortal, Willie Mays sprinting into
and through the ever after, making the catch
that saves the world, then more amazing,
plucking wonder from your glove and whipping it
home with everything you've got, like he did,
ball cap blown from your skull, your living
body splayed then spliced, like his, by joy.

Sean McFadden
HEAVENS TO BETSY

Nolan packed his olive-green suit for his mom's funeral, leaving the black suit in Chicago. Colleen's tiny hands had clung to life for twelve years following a six-month sentence from her oncologists. Existing over that brutal final month on nothing but ice chips and morphine, she died at a gruesome sixty-two pounds. Nolan's relief was too intense to justify wearing black. She would never be in pain again, so he wasn't grieving. Black would have been insincere, and she deserved sincerity. He was certain she would have approved of wearing olive. Late spring was her favorite time of year, with the dogwoods and rhododendron in bloom.

"Olive green makes sense," said his girlfriend Sherri, an artist, as they each packed. "It's a sharp suit. She would have liked seeing you in it. I'll wear black, but that's just me."

Once in Maryland, his family proactively inquired about his fashion sense, and he admitted to olive. They went ballistic and sent his sister-in-law to go help him shop for a black suit in town.

"Help me understand your line of thinking," Diane said, holding up a jacket.

"I'm not sad."

"Well…yeah," she scoffed, stopping just shy of saying, "But you're still among adults." He was twenty-eight.

***

Colleen Clearwater adored babies and Nolan was her last. She doted, keeping her youngest engaged in her world, down to the onion dip she'd leave him in charge of when they had company. The clear superiority of leftover dip convinced Nolan that the sour cream had to be added the night before for proper onion rehydration. She'd rave about how much better his was than her last-minute crunchy version. Any sauce on the stove, she'd have him stirring and tasting, asking his opinion. She made the kitchen so comfortable for him, she set him on his first career path, back of the house in a host of restaurants.

***

His brothers mingled with the crowd inside the funeral home, while Diane tried to placate Nolan's father. Nolan and Sherri were assigned to watch the twins.

Out back beside a deep burgundy Japanese maple, his niece Rowan told Nolan, "I can tie my shoes. Kiley can't." Her twin was off with Sherri.

"I only learned how to tie mine a few days ago," Nolan said. "Just for this."

Rowan's eyebrows raised. She smiled and spun a quarter turn on her heels like a toy, ending up with her back to him, frozen.

"She's broke!" Nolan cried and she giggled.

He wasn't that much older than the twins when his mom took him and a friend to the Executive Suite to get their hair cut by professionals. She let the barbers know she'd be back to pick the boys up after her bowling, handing them over to strangers in smocks. Nolan checked out the magazine pile and saw *Playboy* and one of childhood's great days was underway.

He still told Mom everything, though, so one day during their McDonald's trip after piano, he explained that he'd already seen four centerfolds, which clearly meant he wasn't a little kid anymore, and it might be high time he switched to Big Macs. He never set foot in the Executive Suite again. Colleen cut his hair at home from then on. Through the years her skills grew to the point she could even negotiate all his cowlicks. He came to enjoy the time they'd spend together in the laundry room. She took her time with the cut, and he loved her attention.

He would crank Elvis Costello in his room so they could hear it down the hall while she trimmed, and she'd tell him which songs weren't bad and which ones she couldn't stand. They agreed track for track on *Imperial Bedroom*. The screaming was unnecessary. She even liked some Ramones, or at least the '50s covers from *End of the Century*. While she had him subdued, she taught Laundry 101– not just sorting but rubbing the soap in to get a stain out, how to fold and why to hang shirts damp, warning there wouldn't always be a woman in his life to handle these things. She was born in the mid 1920's, so she was bona fide old school, but nobody could say she was wrong. There most certainly wouldn't be.

✲✲✲

Back before he and Sherri were even dating, he'd bring her up while talking on the phone with his mom—so out of character that Colleen called him on it. He explained the obsessively rewritten letters he'd sent to Sherri months earlier. She was dating someone, but they still bumped into each other at the local dive, and Nolan wanted to make sure he said his piece on his terms. The first letter took seven drafts and was inspired but ignored. A follow-up was also ignored. His mom said, "This one must be pretty special, to have you so riled up. I hope to high heaven I get the chance to meet her."

So did Nolan, but he didn't see how. He had once shared a fumbling moment with Sherri's roommate and wasn't sure if the roommate held a grudge. Nervous that his letters might get tossed, he had typed the envelopes at work and used his office's return address. Sherri, a gifted painter, assumed they were from bill collectors and threw them in a pile on top of her speaker. He continued to bump into her at the bar and feel the familiar soaring heart followed by crushing embarrassment when she'd fail to bring up the letters. Five months crawled by without a word, but to her credit, the day she did open one, she called him at work that afternoon.

"I got your letter."

"Which one?" he asked.

"My God! How many are there?"

"Just two, but I liked the first one more."

"Ok. If you still...We should go out," she said.

"You broke up with what's-his-face?"

"Pretty sure I just did. Long time coming."

✲✲✲

"I considered getting you a letter opener," his mom teased on the day she finally met Sherri. Pulling her in for a big hug she whispered, "Are you a neat person?"

"I think so?" Sherri whispered back.

Nolan was only told about that later by Sherri. He guessed Colleen was warning Sherri that her youngest was a slob, that she hadn't meant "neat" like "swell." Minutes after meeting Sherri,

22

Nolan's father began lecturing her on how artists never make any money while they're alive, so art was fine as a hobby, and Sherri left the room while Oscar was still talking. Nolan's heart pounded and he swallowed a laugh. His mom's opinion was the one that mattered, and during their goodbye hug Colleen whispered, "She's a keeper." Sherri's gram had said the same thing to Sherri after meeting Nolan. Neither woman fished, as far as he knew.

✿ ✿ ✿

"Can I have some?" Rowan pointed at Nolan's flask.

"No, you cannot." He slid it back into the pocket of his black jacket. "We'll find you something better."

The second Nolan got his driver's license he joined his restaurant coworkers for drinks after work. They were each buying rounds, and on Nolan's second turn, he paid the bartender three dollars, which was all he had left as a busboy, then he delivered the tray of drinks himself, but then the bartender started yelling, none of which made sense, so Nolan took a seat and drank while it got sorted. The bartender was angry, but Nolan couldn't have been happier.

Colleen was treated to her son waving his finger in her face at two in the morning, insisting, "I only had one," then staggering down the hall, bouncing off one wall then the other. She stayed up all night, traumatized her seventeen-year-old had driven home in that state. But Nolan assured her the next afternoon that his co-workers had driven and left the car parked out on the road. He had no clue how he'd actually gotten home. Colleen never let him forget the scene. Whenever she saw him with a drink in his hand, she liked to mutter, "I only had one," so no one could hear but him.

She was a prolific letter writer, and her primary concern was his drinking. The letters began in college and didn't stop when he dropped out. Colleen wrote how when she was in school at Immaculata, beer was a privilege they splurged on rarely, and it was a very big deal when they did. Nolan wasn't shocked—a traditional women's Catholic college during World War II didn't sound like a party school, unlike his. Her letters warned of the rampant alcoholism on her side of the family, and how the men had all either died drunk, sobered up, or relapsed and died. While Nolan viewed these anecdotes as curious, he didn't see how they related to him.

❊ ❊ ❊

Once upon a time, the dying Queen had an eternal bachelor son who finally wed and soon fathered identical twin girls. While the infants Rowan and Kiley crawled across the king-sized bed, a light emanated from within the Queen and she explained in a faltering voice to the choked-up crowd of family assembled, "Now I know why I've been sticking around."

The youngest was usurped.

❊ ❊ ❊

"Mom said you have needles and pins," Rowan said.

"Your mom said that?" Nolan asked. "Maybe your mom's projecting."

"Oh?" Rowan looked and sounded rather dubious for a four-year old.

His mom spent her life on pins and needles; her untreated anxiety was off the charts. But her heroines included Carol Burnett and Lucille Ball, and sometimes that showed. At a family wedding in Puerto Rico, the roaches in their refrigerator and the giant flying roaches elsewhere had her flustered beyond normal levels. She called to request an exterminator, but when a maid showed up at the door asking something in Spanish, Colleen answered, "I'm sorry, I don't speak English," and shut the door in the woman's face. She spun around to her stunned family.

"Honest to goodness. Did I just? Oh, fluff...But it wasn't the exterminator! Well, that poor woman has a story to tell. 'Look out for the lady in 412–she doesn't speak English. She'll tell you all about it. In English.'" She wrung her hands. "More exterminators around here, less maids, are what you need." She folded her arms and squinted at the ceiling.

"Do we know what she wanted?" she asked.

"No!" they all cried.

"She's on the other side of the door, Mom," Nolan added, trying to be helpful.

24

"When I was in bed, Tinkerbelle was outside my window," Rowan said. "I didn't let her in." She looked shocked at her decision.

"You didn't want to fly?"

"Oops."

Nolan laughed and tried to imagine any truth behind her story. Early for fireflies. Grandma checking in on her darlings on her way out? Why not?

When Nolan was ten, his mom told him, "I ran into Muhammad Ali at the Cherry Hill Mall. I really did. He knocked me flat on my rear end. I must not have been paying attention...I wasn't. He was walking out, I was walking in, and BANG! A brick wall. He was polite, though, very kind. I was down on my bottom, and he helped me up to my feet. I was all out of sorts, so I just pointed at him and said, 'It's you!' And he smiled and said, 'Yes, it is. Are you certain you're alright, ma'am?' I didn't even think to get an autograph for you until after he and his crowd were gone. I'm so sorry."

She showed him where the heavyweight champ put the hurt on, where her arm was already bruising. His own mom. Nobody at school believed him, but Nolan knew for a fact she'd gone head-to-head with Ali. His mom didn't make up stories.

❀❀❀

Sherri returned from examining birch tree bark with Kiley. "How's everyone doing?"

"Pop Pop's sad," Rowan said, drawing on the pavement with a stick.

Nolan sucked in his breath and he and Sherri exchanged a look.

"Do you want to go visit with him?" Sherri asked.

Rowan nodded, then shook her head, frowning.

"Well. What if you tell me about your drawing? I love what you're doing over here. What did you use for that part?"

Rowan beamed.

Uncertain emotions were going around, which was nothing new. His father had summoned him home to say goodbye to his mom so many times Nolan lost track. Oscar always ended up wrong, but each instance meant pure panic. Nolan would thousand-mile-stare out the plane window, slamming scotch, fretting over what to say that hadn't already been said. Nothing was unsaid. Was he supposed to cry?

Oscar would meet him at the airport and rehash how dire things were. Then Nolan would go sit on her bed and embellish stories about his work and love life and update her on the latest adventures of Nitwit. She'd fallen in love with his spaniel mix the second she heard how he'd buried his head in a fresh snowdrift and popped out with a twenty-dollar bill in his mouth. She implored Nolan to take good care of that dog, as if there were another option. She got on him about his drinking, wanting him to get sober like his uncles had, the ones who lived. She made him promise to stay in touch with family when she was gone. But Colleen looked so rejuvenated by the time he left that Nolan never knew if he had just said goodbye.

On several occasions he took the dreaded flight back to Philly, went straight to her hospital room and just asked her if she wanted to go home. "Yes!" both times. The doctors didn't argue. She'd already proven them overpaid pessimists. He drove his parents back down to Maryland, cooked oxtail stew and fried tomatoes with gravy, chatted with her for hours on end and days later found himself back on a plane, Dewar's and a window, wondering what the hell had just happened.

At the end, with the ice-chip diet underway and the unforgivable crime of Colleen's skull defining her features, the days crawled past while they surrounded her bed, and Nolan had quiet words with God for not intervening. Such pointless suffering was okay with her Creator why, exactly? As days grew to weeks, he and his brothers had to return to work. Nolan flew back to Chicago, where his answering machine never flashed any mercy from God's corner. One particularly drunken evening waiting for the phone to ring, he snapped, destroying his furniture, and was fortunate nobody in the building called the cops. By the time he was done, there was so much broken wood, the apartment smelled like a campfire ready to light.

"God's got a plan?" he yelled at the splintered futon frame and busted table. "For her life, all seventy pounds of life there? Fuck God. And fuck that plan!"

❊ ❊ ❊

After a month of watching Colleen waste away, her husband found the necessary balls and told her it was time, that he was ready, and she let go that very instant, showing her cards at last–just waiting for that man all along.

The phone call wasn't urgent. The clock had stopped. The flight out east wasn't nerve-wracking, and the suit he packed wasn't black. It was over.

Nolan had never attended a happier funeral, even if he remained outside through most of it. Everyone he met seemed relieved. They all skipped past sadness. The service was more about celebrating life before the term became commonplace.

A closed casket made even more space for photos, and he was allowed one to sit on top. He chose the Hollywood shot where she was dancing under a massive chandelier in a stately ballroom of the Q.E. II back in the early 80's. Stunning in a lustrous black sequined evening gown and long black gloves, a cross between Claudette Colbert and Elizabeth Taylor, hamming it up with a rose in her teeth, she stretched her arms out towards a white-tuxedoed Oscar, the love of her life, so clear by the look in her eyes.

🐾 🐾 🐾

Kiley pulled Sherri away to show her an egg she'd discovered under the pungent boxwood hedge. Nolan gave Rowan the high sign and she shadowed him inside the funeral home where he'd hoped to show his face and grab a drink he didn't have to sneak. His flask was empty, and he hadn't realized the funeral had no bar.

"You remind me of someone," he told Rowan.

"My sister?" she sighed. "Everybody always…"

"Nope."

Rowan frowned, popping a finger in her ear. "Who?"

Nolan pointed to a picture of a very young Colleen, playing in the sand "down the shore," probably Cape May.

"My mom. Your grandma."

Rowan smiled at the photo then squinted. "Grandma?"

"Yeah. You favor her."

"I'll do a favor for grandma."

"You already are. You're keeping me company."

"Mmm. She died." Rowan pointed her foot out at him, still laced.

Nolan swallowed. "She did. So, uh, you've got to show me which knot you used."

"It's easy," she said. "But wait till Kiley gets back."

"Sure, sure. Don't want to waste an opportunity to help your sister."

Rowan nodded sleepily, smiling, understood.

Diane popped out of the crowd to check on them.

"Don't you two look nice," she said. She kissed her daughter on the head then adjusted Nolan's cuffs, so they'd stick out more under the black jacket.

"Sorry, this is taking so long...ugh. You know what I mean. Bet you never knew you were such a good babysitter. Any chance you still got this one?"

"Uh-huh," Nolan and Rowan said in unison.

Rowan anchored her little hand around her uncle's index finger. Nolan froze and smiled.

"She's got me," he admitted, the words catching like crunchy bits of dried onion in his throat. He looked down at her tiny fingers hanging on.

Richard Rubin
FLYING

What is it about the birds
tucked in limbs and leaves,
a canvas flourishing with yellows and greens
the light brushed out through the branches?
       They look out,
       the face of strangers.

If I had wings
I would wrap them tight around me
snug in my own body heat
and let the others fly.
       I am the old man in the peeling house
       coming out only at night when no one is looking.

Cicadas rev and ebb,
fireflies drift in aimless incandescence.
All the birds are black now
turning colors only in the morning light.
       I want to hear them--
       the thwap of mourning dove wings.

I don't really care for walking in the woods
I am not dawn or dusk.
My hands make a nest
but the spirits have vanished from its cup.
       My limbs are filled with birds
       all ready to fly.

John Davis
RUNNING GAME

Whole years I knew only strides: streets
and dry trails, the rocky dust steep

with coyotes and snakes. Venom lingered
like a weathervane waiting for wind.

I ran. The breathing of leaves eased my breathing.
I ran from the edges of land tracing

tomorrow in strained circles, my shoes
worn down from blue gravity those days

I was a guest in scrub pine rhythms.
Afternoons shadowed my skin from

vein to leg vein. Where the canyon
blended with the creek and layers of smog,

I ran my skeleton the way you run a horse
training for a race not knowing the race

was already in me, the finish line ahead always
ahead in what has died and what survives.

Jenna Le
LINEA NIGRA

linea nigra, noun. *A dark vertical line that appears on the abdomen during pregnancy.*

The doctors, babbling in Latin
as is their wont, style you black,
but I see you as you are:
a muddy purplish-brown,
smudgy like squashed mosquito viscera
or like plum juice
smeared on leather pants.

If I could contort my body
and press my ear to your skinny
musteline length, I'd hear
a continuous low-pitched
electric hum, almost
too quiet to be detectable,
like seismographic activity
near a faultline,
sometimes broken by a violent
splash, thrash, or thwack.

Also: intermittent burbling,
as one hears beside a pond
with a frog in it.

You smell like a couch
with decades of sweat
baked into it, also
the chemical odor
of an animal hormone
excitable and feral,
an unfamiliar ink, a fountain pen
bought in a dreamed-up country.

Phillip Sterling
SELECTED STORIES OF EUDORA WELTY

```
┌─────────────────────────────────────────────┐
│                                               │
│           Presented as a gift to the          │
│       KENTWOOD BRANCH LIBRARY                  │
│                  by the                        │
│            Kentwood Women's Club               │
│                   1997                         │
│                                               │
└─────────────────────────────────────────────┘
```

DATE DUE

JUL 30 1997 [Checked out by Kentwood Women's Club President
Rosemary Gleason on July 16, the day the book appeared on the
library's "New Arrivals" table. Rosemary made it a point to check out
every book the KWC provided funds for, in the belief that any book
without a due date stamped in it was doomed to early withdrawal,
given the reluctance on the part of the city to move forward with
the proposed library expansion. (There was not enough space in the
old building, she'd argued repeatedly, particularly since magazines
could no longer be stored in the mold-infested basement.) Rosemary
felt the gesture was imperative in her role as KWC president, not to
mention her civic duty as wife of Harold Gleason, Jr., two-term city
commissioner and Vice Chair of the city's Library Committee.

Besides, Rosemary loved to read. She'd attended Central
Michigan University as an English major, but switched to
Administrative Assistant/Legal Secretarial upon Harold's graduation
and subsequent marriage proposal. Harold was four years her
senior, three years ahead of her in school. They'd met at a Sigma Chi
party her freshman year (when she called herself Rose Marie out of
deference to some romantic notion of literary tradition). She'd recalled
reading "The Worn Path" in her Intro to Lit course at CMU, but now,
so many years later, found herself unable to maintain much interest in
many of Welty's other stories and so returned the book to circulation
well before its due date. Just the same, Rosemary recommended the
book (with tempered enthusiasm, as she was wont to do) at the next
regular meeting of the KWC.]

AUG 19 1997 [Checked out on August 5 by Julie VanDyke, KWC Vice President, upon recommendation of Rosemary Gleason. Julie publicly admitted she was "not much of a reader," beyond a seasonal indulgence in articles from the flower and horticulture magazines she received as a member of the Kentwood Garden Club, to which she also belonged. But *Selected Stories* wouldn't be like reading a whole novel, would it? Welty's stories were short, for the most part, and didn't many of them take place in Mississippi, where Julie was born and lived for the first two years of her life? Not that she could remember. Her family had moved North, relocating to Flint, when her father, trained by the Army as a mechanical engineer, got a job with General Motors. Some few years later, executive buy-outs at GM and generous tax-incentives from the City of Kentwood provided her father with the wherewithal to venture into the manufacturing world on his own, the result of which was MX Stamping, a tool and die company founded specifically to service the aeronautic and automobile industries, one of the first publicly traded companies in the greater Grand Rapids area to be majority owned by an African American.

It was for somewhat personal reasons as well, then, that Julie — as the daughter of former Mississippian Louis R. Johnson (VanDyke is her married name) — took the initiative to check out the book Rosemary Gleason had recommended. Julie got no further in her reading than the word "n---"[1] — at which point she closed the book decidedly and returned it to the library.]

SEP 05 1997 [Checked out on August 22 by Adrienne Sykesma, mother of Nancy ("Nan") Sykesma, a Ph.D. student at Michigan State University who, with her eighteen-month-old son Haby (Ferdosi), was living in her childhood home in Kentwood so that Adrienne could watch Haby while Nan prepared for her comprehensive exams in Twentieth Century American Literature. (Nan was ABD, but had yet to declare a dissertation topic; one title she'd been playing with was "The Tolling of Southern Belles: Death as Prototypical Male in Carson McCullers, Flannery O'Connor, and Eudora Welty"). *Selected Stories* was not only prominent on the recommended reading list provided by the Chair of Graduate Studies for the Department of English but also available in the Kent District Library System. In fact, Adrienne found thirteen of the

---

1   The editors note the author's intent to quote Welty as she wrote the phrase, but to not continue the harm caused by that word.

books on her daughter's reading list available in the system, which would therefore save Nan several hours of driving back and forth to MSU's library in East Lansing.]

SEP 20 1997 [Check out renewed by Adrienne Sykesma on September 6—within the 24-hour grace period that allowed a waiver of late fees—since Nan had gotten behind in her reading, due in part to Haby's chronic ear infection and fever, in part to the incident with Haby's dad in the courtroom during the custody hearing (*How could Nan possibly concentrate now?!*), and in part to Brent ("Sully") Sullivan, who Nan had met at Bar 84 in Byron Center one of the nights she'd gone there to study for her exams "in peace and quiet."

It was October 19 by the time Adrienne finally returned the book (with several others) to the Kentwood Branch of the Kent District Library System—three days after Nan left for Colorado, where Sully had taken a job driving for UPS (seasonal, at first, but "likely" to become full time). Until Family Court decided otherwise (or Nan's circumstances changed), Haby would stay with Adrienne, his maternal grandmother, who lived within one hundred miles of Haby's dad. Adrienne remitted $11.40 in late fees for the overdue books.]

APR 29 1998 [Checked out on April 15 by Tyler Pearce, a senior at East Kentwood High School. At the time, Tyler was in love. During his spring break in Boca Raton not two weeks before, he had "hooked up with" Dorota Kutnik, a twenty-two-year-old Polish exchange student attending Florida Atlantic University (under a reciprocal agreement with Marie Curie-Skłodowska University in Lublin). Dorota was tall and quiet, a bookish, stereotypical English major (in Tyler's eyes), seemingly oblivious to her natural beauty. She could also legally buy beer. To impress her, Tyler claimed to be in college as well—"part-time, at GRCC"—and while he hadn't decided on a major yet, he'd given a lot of thought to English. After all, Mrs. Vandermark, his tenth-grade English teacher, had liked a number of the haiku he'd written during the poetry unit.

The couple shared email addresses and promised to stay in touch. Tyler thought maybe they'd find a way to spend some time together come summer. Dorota thought Tyler could maybe help proofread and edit her literature papers, the next being on *Death of a Salesman.*

"The play or the short story?" asked Mrs. Diddle, the Kentwood librarian. When Tyler guessed "story," he was directed to Eudora Welty's "Death of a Traveling Salesman."

By the thirteenth exchange of the young lovers' emails, Tyler realized he'd made a mistake. They didn't look to be compatible.]

JUN 29 1998 [Checked out on June 15 by Bernice Salazar, who had joined the Kentwood Women's Club in May, having taken a job as branch manager of the Fifth Third Bank on 28th Street. The book was on the prior year's list of the club's donations, which Bernie ("Please") had received from Julie VanDyke, the newly elected President. Bernie enjoyed "lighter" reading during the summer — shorter things — that could be consumed during the rare inactive Sunday afternoon, which was usually all the time she could spare. People didn't realize how busy banks were in the summer, with housing starts and mortgage transfers . . . She didn't have time for blockbuster novels.

While President VanDyke had earmarked *Selected Stories* of Eudora Welty as one of the books she "didn't particularly care for, given the language," such notation was, for a free-thinking, independent Black woman like Bernie Salazar (three divorces in eleven years) the best recommendation anyone could give.]

No further dates are stamped on the circulation sheet glued to the frontispiece of the book. Withdrawn from circulation in 2019 — after it was discovered wedged behind a dozen Kurt Vonnegut books on the bottom shelf of the "Literary Fiction" section of Kentwood's decade-old Media Center expansion — this particular Modern Library edition of *Selected Stories of Eudora Welty* was purchased for $1 from the Friends of the Library by a retired English professor, who added it to the stack of "classics" he intends to return to eventually, given enough time.

Connor Beeman
SONG FOR CHILDHOOD (SONG FOR THE BOYS)

I know boys who've screamed in empty parking lots,
who've let cracked pavement and crabgrass swallow them whole.

boys who've ate through their ration of promises,
who've binged white noise, mixed it with Percocet.

boys who've smashed in the glass of rusting cars
for fun, for kicks, for no reason at all.

I know boys who've become nothing,
become whole, become empty—

who've done it over and over again.

cycle—waves against the rocks,
grey water ever-lapping at the stony shore.

lifted pills, and the friend who told me
he pushes his car to 90

on midnight streets,
just to see what will happen.

fists, blood
and rust.

when I was a boy
  (if I was ever a boy)

I made friends with the trees.

red maple, pine,
the sweet gum in the backyard.

I collected spiked burrs like currency,
loot piled under the porch—a dragon's horde.

I preferred the quiet things.

the sway of branches and leaves,
the wind. birdsong.

at 12, I watched the other boys charge
at each other across a field.

I watched a friend's collarbone shatter—
heard it crack like gunshot in a winter wood.

I realized then that there are things
I cannot lay claim to.

when I go home, the streets whisper the names
of boys I have forgotten.

I try to listen,
but hear taunts instead.

I don't know if I can still speak the language of men.

I don't know if I ever truly spoke it.

in the dining room, the table crowded with expired coupons,
my mother gives me a report of the living,
  the dead, the lost.

out the window—there are still the trees.
the burrs, crowding the porch,
  waiting to be collected.

Divyasri Krishnan
INDUSTRIOUS ANGELS
After Emily Dickinson

They were now on six days of not speaking. New routines substituted themselves for the old. They still woke up in tandem, but where there had once been drowsy greetings there was now only the rustle of sheets, the *sweet-sweet* of birds calling in the morning. In the sour fluorescence of the little bathroom, they stood beside each other in near-perfect silence, accompanied only by the scraping of bristles against enamel.

There was no animosity in their movements; it had been entirely concentrated into the not-speaking. So as he got dressed, Madhumita made him the customary bowl of cornflakes, the bread with a little butter and jam, the cut apple. This he ate as she went to wake Ajay for preschool. At seven, he pulled on his coat, for the weather in California had acquired a light chill to which he was not yet accustomed, and as she handed him his bag, he leaned in automatically to kiss her cheek.

She stilled, her first acknowledgement that something was different between them. Then, slowly, she shook her head.

An apology rose immediately to his lips, but he knew it would only be another affront, disrespecting the precious silence that had become synonymous with her dignity in this fight. So he took the bag, turned, and stepped out the door.

As he drove the twenty minutes to the Motorola office, it occurred to him that the situation they were in was particular to their time. By which he meant that they could not have maintained this lonely, distant togetherness any earlier in their relationship, as they would not have established their routines well enough to conduct them in silence, nor any later, as they would have become too used to each other to lapse so suddenly into strangeness. In fact, it was very possible that he and Madhumita could go forever like this—never speaking, yet working in perfect harmony, until all his remaining hair had fallen, until her softness had folded and spotted, until Ajay was enough of a man that their little apartment no longer meant home.

It was a bleak, claustrophobic prospect. He resolved at once to put an end to it. He would have to do it in a way that sacrificed neither his manhood nor her secret pride, and so transition them easily back to the husband-and-wife business at which they were meant to play.

At the office he kept to himself. The work for which all the great tech companies of the nineties had summoned half of India's college-educated population was lonely by nature. They had given him an ID, a cubicle that was little more than a plastic box, and a desktop. With this he conducted his work, the small magic of an industry they had once said was going to change the world.

By one o'clock he began to get hungry. As he packed up his bag, the scraping of the zipper seemed unforgivably loud. There was a quiet particular to corporate offices—not even really quiet, but a persistent, low-level white noise of churning fans, creaking swivel chairs, and the muted robotic beeps of the fax machine—that created a unique sense of utter and complete estrangement. *Surgical*, he would have called it, except that when one examined the place closely, the carpets, the windowsills, one would find dirt and filth equal to the underbellies of the most poorly maintained autorickshaws.

In Bangalore, how had it been? He remembered the office having many of the same fixtures—the cubicles, the water bubblers—but the feeling being entirely different. Despite the mild temperatures, every window was cracked open, letting in a flood of whirring bicycles, blaring horns, the hiss-sigh of buses pulling into the stop, the fluted voices of students from the nearby all-girls school and the answering laughs of the boys who always waited outside their gate. Lunch, when it came, was long. The whole team, some fifteen engineers of various ages, would leave together and sample the wares of the little stalls that lined the street: bhajji and filter coffee, flaky veg puffs, chaats jeweled with many-colored chutneys. Loneliness was an impossible luxury. All day his ear chimed with someone's thoughts, complaints, noontime prayers. He relished the peace of leaving the office in the evening, but by the time he arrived on his scooter at the boutique startup where Madhumita worked, he was glad to have her honeyed voice occupy his ear once more.

Now he made his way down the quiet hallway which led to the quiet and too-large cafeteria, meeting no one.

A bulbous black television was fixed at an angle in one corner of the cafeteria, painting the tables directly below it in the faint red-green glow of the stock review. These days, it was mostly red. Numbers flashed across the screen, accompanied by very delayed subtitles for whatever the smart, suited analyst of the day was saying.

He watched it while eating his lukewarm pasta marinara, taking in nothing. Instead, he thought about Madhumita and their fight. He couldn't remember what it had been about. The scene itself was a vague unpleasantness in the back of his mind. They were a lucky couple, all things considered; in five years of marriage, he could count the number of big fights they'd had on one, maybe two hands. In the first two years, they had not fought once, even during the difficult third trimester of her pregnancy. He remembered a certain careful, eggshell politeness, the extreme acquiescence one might expect between roommates rather than newlyweds. In a sense they were roommates. He had only met her a week before their wedding. Such was the benefit of arranged marriage — compromise was easy between strangers with no way out.

Maybe he could buy her flowers. No, he amended, spearing a piece of penne, flowers were too expensive, and impractical besides. He could hear her already: *What am I supposed to do with these? Which vase do you expect me to put these in? Or will you go and waste on a new vase as well?*

Or maybe she would say nothing. Her fine, small mouth folding into itself, a neat line, the stitches invisible but the seam strong.

He knew what she would really want. It was what she had wanted for the last four years, and receiving it would erase every wrongdoing he had committed in her eyes. She had not worked since that startup in Bangalore, since she had given birth to Ajay and he had packed up their little unit and brought them to California. For four years she had been sustained only by an offhand comment his boss, a Greek named Nikolaos, had made on his first day: *The way the market's going, we'll be able to upgrade you to an L1 before your boy hits kindergarten.*

The L1 visa was the pipe dream of all immigrants. It meant they could stay here for seven years instead of the maximum six allotted by the H1B, and they could apply for permanent residency without violating the terms of their visa. Most importantly, it meant that Madhumita could finally work again.

He finished his pasta. On the TV, the analyst was yelling at another analyst against a backdrop of flashing graphs. It was settled; at the end of the work day, he would ask Nikolaos about the L1. After all, Ajay would start kindergarten in less than a year.

He worked until six-thirty, by which time the entire floor had emptied and half of the lights had been shut off. In the partial darkness, he powered off his desktop and packed up all his materials: the little college-ruled notebook he used to jot down code, two pens, an empty granola bar wrapper. He made sure to brush all of the brown crumbs into the small dustbin, then, on second thought, unhooked the trash bag and tied the handles together. On his way out, he threw it into the larger communal garbage disposal.

Nikolaos had a corner office on the other end of the floor. His was the only light in a line of black and shuttered doors; since he had started at Motorola fourteen years ago, he had never once left before seven.

The door was open, but he still knocked.

"Come in."

He did.

"Prakash," said Nikolaos, barely turning his head from his computer screen. "Sit down. I'm sending an email."

Prakash sat in one of the gray cushioned chairs that faced Nikolaos and his desk. The Greek man was nearly seven feet, and easily over 200 pounds. Prakash had never seen men so large before coming to America. It could have been something in the food, though that didn't explain the height. So maybe it was something in the air.

Nikolaos powered off his desktop and stretched, his arms like twin skyscrapers, the ceiling entirely too close to his fingertips. He settled them on the desk and fixed Prakash with large, pale eyes.

"I'm glad you came in," he said. "I've been meaning to talk to you."

"I as well, sir," said Prakash.

"How is—Madhu? And the boy?"

"Both very well, sir."

"Good, good."

They were silent for a beat. Then they both spoke at once.

"Sir—"

"I wanted to—"

Both stopped, embarrassed.

"Sorry," Nikolaos said, in the way that meant he wanted to go first. Prakash nodded.

"I wanted to say," the Greek man continued, "that I've really valued your work over the past few years. Your people are really very good at what you do. I've never seen a harder working set." He held up an enormous hand to stop Prakash's response. "That's what makes this so hard. You've seen the news, I presume."

Prakash thought of the analyst in the suit, the cold pasta. The zigzag graphs.

"It's just been bad times on top of bad times for tech right now. We thought the market would bounce back and it just hasn't. So we've got to protect the bottom line. You understand?"

Above them, the fan whirred. The computer hummed. The chair's flimsy plastic joints groaned under Prakash's shifting weight.

"We're letting you go."

Then he was in the parking lot, in the car, the lights blurring the night indistinct, then he was turning into the apartments at Lawrence and 1st. The windows of the third floor glowed yellow. If he counted, he could pick out which one belonged to them. It was the window that looked into their bedroom, Ajay's Spongebob bed right under the sill where it received the most light in the morning.

He didn't know how long he sat in the car, staring into nothing, but by the time he came to, only a few lights were still on. Theirs was not one of them. He checked his watch; it was almost eleven o'clock.

Eleven o'clock on December 27th, 2001. A year after the dot com bubble burst in earnest, three months after the fall of the Twin Towers, a week after Motorola announced it would be laying off 9,400 workers, a significant percentage of whom were H1B workers brought over in the frenzy of the internet boom, and who would now be given all of two months to find another job or leave the country.

He realized he was hungry. Between lunch and now he had only eaten the one granola bar. He thought of how carefully he'd cleaned his desk, how he'd taken out the trash. He had meant to do it as a model employee, one deserving of an L1. Only now did he realize that he had cleared out his desk for unemployment.

As he rode the elevator up to the third floor, he tried to quell the rumblings of his stomach, but couldn't—and wasn't it ridiculous, downright insensitive, for his stomach to demand anything when he had lost everything? For the functions of the body to continue their cruel cycle even while the world was ending? He opened the door to the dark apartment, doing his best to be quiet, determined not to let Madhumita know the next morning he had gone without dinner, for she was sure to scold him.

But there she was, sitting at the kitchen table. She was so still he almost did not see her. In the light through the half-opened door, he could make out the sweet crescent of her face, the glint of gold at her neck that was the chain her mother had given her before they had left Bangalore, the red bottu that punctuated the center of her smooth forehead.

They watched each other like this, him at the door, her at the table. Then he shut the door behind him, cutting off the stream of light, and spoke into the new blackness.

"I lost my job."

She was quiet for some time. He didn't move, didn't say anything more, only strained to see what he could of her in the faint light, trying to make out anything of the expressions that had over these few years become so dear to him.

At last she rose from the table and moved to the fridge. As she opened the door, her face was thrown into sharp relief by the cold blue light, the warmth of her skin suddenly washed out. She retrieved a small Tupperware container from inside and closed the door, receding once again into darkness as she made her way towards him.

He took the container, which was almost too cold to touch, and opened it. The familiar smell of tamarind, curry leaves, and chili powder drifted up to him. He didn't even need the light to know what it was; the back of his throat tightened in hungry recognition. She had made small onion vathakozhambu, a specialty from their hometowns in Tamil Nadu. It had been four years since he'd last tasted it.

He looked into her eyes, circles of black impossibly darker than their surroundings. "Madhu," he said softly, "we might have to—"

"Chup," she said, the chiding gentle, sweet. "Just eat."

Matt Thomas
FOR ALBERT HAWKINS, WHOM THE STATE HAS LABELED A HOARDER

His works and wonders are pennies to wedge into each blown fuse
to keep the lights on at any cost, a fire trap, what they will say,
not seeing the house for the acrid tendrils of what if,
the collection of doors like trailheads, rooms natural wonders.
As if moderation could be at home, when home is a bottomless word.
But that, and that, and that call a question so nearly right
that surely some next thing will be the what that knows what to ask,
each query an acquisition of a mote, dinner eaten above the bedrock answer
on a scavenged table made three legged by ankle threatening regolith.
What birth doesn't sore the eyes, isn't terrible?
His squalling rust, rot, mildew: energies decoding our promise
beneath the escaped, writhing byproduct of that combustion:
a snow of old receipts, newspapers, yellowed mail, steel, glass, plastic, rubber;
the whiskered, nicotined, shoveler sweating shirtless before the furnace.
Look at yourself as you pass by, there in the hoarder Albert Hawkins.

Ken Hines
CAREER PATH

What got to me wasn't the overturned trailer, helpless
as a turtle on its back or the Keystone Kop snaring
of fugitive pigs, not even the bristled hero
who squirted through authority's grasp. But soon as it flashed
on my phone — *Trailer loaded with hogs overturns on I-95,
all but one recovered* —

I saw myself, drowsing on the Third St. Express
as it barrelled down the freeway jam-packed
with my compatriots, soon to be herded
into waiting office towers. When the bus leaned

into a turn, I found myself wanting the driver
to floor it and cut the wheel hard, blowing up rows of
bollards and barriers, imagining lanyard-yoked passengers
vaulting through broken windows as the eerie yowl of sirens
announced the arrival of EMTs. As stunned commuters

posted videos and texts from the safety of the shoulder,
I'd climb over the chain link fence, head foggy, blood
crusting my face. And I'd think about the news that night:
driver discharged from the hospital, all passengers treated
and released, except for one nameless worker no one has seen.

Russell Thorburn
THE LAST PLACE ON EARTH IN MEXICO CITY

The fix-it guy wearing a faded eggshell colored
cap cracks his melody maker from its case
to play his high-pitched teardrop of a note.
Everything I do is to improve the sound,
Franciso mutters with a cigarette chumped
down on his lower lip, wheezing more
of his accordion that he's repairing today
between his sunspotted hands of sixty.
His eyes are of the night without sleep,
blowing leaves across an empty plaza,
forlorn calls of his empty stomach
as his fingers try to burst open a melody.
His slender figure of a man who's still in his prime
leans his cheek a certain way that tells
of a woman not yet forgotten, as his eyes roll back
in this lost tango loved by Jewish Iraqis
and Arab orchestras. His hips torn one way
while the rest of his body complains that
it can't follow his feet on such an unimportant morning
as this, the whiskey bottle full enough on a table
beside broken accordions like his Excelsior,
white as a snowy owl that roosts on the floor.
But Francisco suddenly stops as if seeing death
in the corner of his Mexico City music repair shop,
those buskers and maestros of an exhausted earth
on their way to the graveyard despite
little resurrections made by men like him.

Diane Payne
PROSPECT PARK: A HAIBUN SERIES

In elementary school, we were expected to walk home from school for lunch every day, yet I always wondered if I packed a lunch and ate at the park, if I'd meet the men who built furniture at Baker's Furniture Factory. I was certain that they'd enjoy their lunch break beneath a large oak tree, admiring trees the way they admired the wood they used to make furniture. Unlike General Motors, where my dad worked, this factory was quiet, and the workers didn't seem rushed. They'd stand by the window and wave to me. They probably didn't race to the bar to get drunk when their shift ended like at GM.

Noon horn blasts in town
Chat over thermos of soup
Laughter beneath trees

On special days, some of our teachers, the ones who appreciated trees and fresh air, would walk with us to the park and they'd sit on a bench while we climbed the monkey bars, wishing we could climb the tall trees instead, which made our teachers too nervous. After school, I'd walk directly to the park. I had my favorite trees and I was certain they were waiting for me. Then I'd walk home to get my dog, bring him to the park, and he'd be so thrilled to be outside, we'd walk around all the trees, me telling one story after another beneath the shade of the trees, dog loyally at my side.

Dog circles the trees
Smells the bark, then digs the ground
Branches reach to dog

One night, somehow, a beautiful coffee table made from Baker's Furniture Factory appeared next to our back door. Instead of being happy, my mother demanded that my father return this table.

"Everyone will know you stole it," she hissed.

"I didn't steal it!" my father screamed.

"You sure as hell didn't pay for it. What kind of table just appears in the middle of the night?"

"It's a gift. For you. I'm trying to be nice."
By this point in life, we knew how wedding rings and cars appeared and disappeared, and we knew to never ask our dad if he won or lost playing poker, because when he lost, he was not only a badly hungover dad, but a very angry dad.

Mahogany tree
Crafted into a table
No one understands

My dad's poker friend, who lived behind us, worked at Baker's, and he must have found a way to sneak into the factory at night and drop this table off by our door before morning. From that day on, this table sat in our dingy living room, looking very out of place, until my mother decided to balance things out by placing her Bible, that she never read, but it's where she wrote down her family tree, on the center of that table. She polished that wood until she died. I always wondered if those men waving to me while I sat beneath a maple tree in Prospect Park knew their table ended up in our run-down house, and if furniture had a way of routinely disappearing during the night, while the tall trees provided a quiet cover to thievery, and how these trees may have not only felt relieved, but revered, that they stood tall while the other trees became tables and chairs.

Trees retain memory
Leaves carry vivid stories
Shared life with live trees

Matt Thomas
OPEN CARRY

A dogwood petal lands on a sleeve,

a starling angles just so as to brush a bare shoulder.

Why do we shrug when the world comforts itself?

It's as good as a caress of the limbs we used to have.

This dude at the feed store eyed my look as if a curse

and reached to touch the grip of a Glock

to ward off the uncertainty of my intention.

All I can think, the ugly butt of that metal

how good it feels in the hand

maybe as good as the weight of petals, birds.

Flip the visor to that little vanity mirror

and see a glint,

maybe energy singing in the dark,

a song in your eye

about the terrible softness of our bodies.

Matt Dennison
COLD METAL PART

I worked in the Texas oil fields
when young enough to climb
rain-slick tanks and lift live wires
so the trucks could pass while the others
stood and watched. Oh, it was good—
feet willingly grounded in permanent
adulthood, if need be, where I met Preston,
the old black mechanic who would,
they all said, paint your house for
ten bucks and a bottle of whiskey.
A strong and kindly man, he helped
me with my confusing first-job tasks:
the changing of giant tires with the
sledgehammer drop and the staring
down of drivers of failed inspections
while the others stood and watched
and I remember Preston making a
cold metal part when none was available
or yet invented and realizing there would be
solutions in this world—and Preston
at the company Christmas party,
rough in his blue suit smiling
just inside the door after winning
the grand prize drawing of
twenty dollars after twenty-one
years of labor and his laughter
growing and building until
breaking then suddenly
sobbing forth into
silence.

Zackary Medlin
TRAPLINES

The surface of last week's snow melts a bit every day then refreezes at night, forms a filigree of ice that crunches with each step. It's easy to get lost in that sound, that slight resistance before it crushes beneath you. So satisfying. We've spent the morning breaking trail out to the Chatanika to check the traps. Jacob's been itching to go after seeing all these Alaska shows on TV, the ones where you've got to kill the world before it kills you. And, after watching that crap, I guess it's time for him to see it for what it is. He's too eager to kill.

Jacob's steps stop, and it's that sudden absence of sound that pulls me out of myself and back into the now. The black water is already visible in the center of the river. Makes it dangerous. The ice we can see is being cut back beneath, leaving an icy arch without a keystone. Means we've got to take our time, probe the snow to find where the bank ends. Otherwise, you walk out on that edge and something bad is bound to happen. But Jacob isn't looking at the water. I turn and he's looking to the sky. He sees me and points up at the shape wheeling above us.

"Raven," he says, but it's a question. He wouldn't have stopped if he really thought it was a raven.

"Too big. What's that mean?" I ask him.

"Eagle?"

"Yep. You know how else you can tell? See those little feathers at the end of his wings, the ones that look like fingers? They're called winglets. There's winglets on planes too, but we got the idea from them," I say, pointing up. "You don't see many this far inland."

"How come he's here?"

"See how he's still all brown, doesn't have his white head yet? Means he's young. In winters like this, there's not enough food for them all. See, when you see an animal, what you're really seeing is hunger; they're made of it. It's what keeps them moving, keeps them alive, but the real young ones and real old ones have to work a bit harder for it."

❊

Jacob hears it first, coming from the slough where grayling and whitefish post up in spring, upriver from the pike and close to open water in case those pike get starved curious. The sound's about thirty or forty feet off, a mewling interrupted by huffs gone gravelly from pain and time. I give the hood of his parka a little tug. When he looks up, my finger's already up over my lips. I put my palm flat to his chest while I slide in front, the same way Dad did when we stumbled up on that grizzly in Valdez. Everything was fine then, probably is now, too, but when there's hurt involved —

"Stay here. Be still. I mean it."

I wait until I'm a little farther from the boy to unholster my Colt .22. I chamber a round and push through the alder. It's not easy or quiet moving, and whatever's howling hears. I still can't see it through the brush, but when it hisses, I'm sure it's a lynx.

There's no good way to do this. I grab a limb from the ground and toss it behind the sound. The lynx startles out of the brush, pulling hard against a trap that's got no business being where it is. The thing thrashes until its broken fibula tears through the meat and skin. All that stuff about animals chewing their own legs off's mostly bullshit. Takes too much thought. That's a plan. No, when folks find a leg left in a trap it's usually been torn loose from the thing ripping itself away from its body. Like this one's trying to do. That's when I fire.

"D-dad?" There's a quaver in his voice.

"Everything's fine, buddy. I'm—"

"Did ya kill it? What is it? Can I see?"

"Pump your brakes, boy. It isn't something good. This," I nod toward the lynx, "this is the aftermath of an asshole." He smirks a little at hearing his dad swear. "It's not a bad word when it's the right word." This seems like the kind of time to tussle his hair, but between his hood and his cap, that seems cumbersome, so I just pull his wool cap down over his eyes the way he hates for me to do. He thinks he's too old for it. Only a few months ago his mom was in tears because he leaned away from her goodbye kiss that morning. I don't blame him. Starting middle school is rough enough around here without the older kids thinking you're a "mama's boy." But he's a good enough kid that I know he'll regret it one day, so there's no reason to make him feel bad about it now.

When he pulls that cap back up, I step aside and let him have a minute with the animal. After all, they do look cool, like wizards, the way their guard hairs tuft up into sharp little points at the ears and the fringe around their mouths hangs like a cartoonish mustache. If it weren't for paws the size of a man's fist, and the claws they hide, they'd hardly strike you as dangerous, unless you've seen what pain and fear bring out. See, most times, you won't even know a lynx was there, you'll just be missing a chicken. But if it's angry, say some rooster got its spur in the thing, well, then you've got a mess. That's when you see what they really are.

"Dad, why's this trapper an asshole?"

"Because he doesn't know what he's doing, and that's unacceptable. When what you're doing is killing, you need to mean it. You need to have intent. Look here at this trap."

"Looks the same as one of yours."

"Yep; it's a three-thirty. He's using a small game trap out on a big game trail. Did you notice there weren't any other tracks? Means he hasn't checked his traps since the last snow. No telling how long it's been caught up and hurting."

"So, since he didn't come back…can I skin it? My scout book showed me how, like helping it out of a sweater."

"That what it said? No, we aren't going to skin it; it's not our kill. And no, skinning's not taking off a sweater. I don't want you thinking about it that way. Jacob, this is important. This lynx was alive; now it's not. Someone made that happen. I was saving this for your first hunt, that's when my dad gave me this talk, but I guess now's as good a time as any."

I kneel next to the cat to free it from the trap and start laying it out for the cutting. It feels both wrong and familiar. Jacob's old enough to handle this. Right? I grew up with kids that were hunting alone at eleven. Times change, though. But it's too late to turn back now, I suppose.

"When we kill something, it's not fun, and it's not like the movies. I'm not going to smear blood on your face and call you a man. And when we dress it out, we sure as hell aren't going to pretend we're taking off a sweater. We respect what we do by doing it our way. The whole 'sweater' thing is to help people get comfortable with the killing, but maybe this isn't something we're supposed to get comfortable with. Here, take my knife, I want you to try something."

"But I've got my own." Jacob pulls his hand out of his mitten to reach for his belt.

"I know, but we're saving that one for when we do it proper. For now, I want you to take mine." I take his hand in mine, feel it tremble. So small. "Push it in the belly, right here. Go deep."

"That's not how you —"

"I know, son. Do it anyway."

"This is how your dad taught you?"

"More or less."

Jacob pushes the blade. The skin resists at first, but when it gives, the blade slips deep, until his little hand's pressed against the cat's fur and slicked with blood. I wrap my hand around his and we draw the knife through the belly until his hand slides away and it's just me opening the lynx to the ground. Short steps crunch the snow behind me. When I look back, he's pressed against the alders with his hands shoved deep in his coat pockets.

"Okay, Jacob. Look here, look at me. It's okay to cry, to close your eyes, even to get sick. I just want you to feel this. This is natural, the things your body's doing." I kneel down, take my gloves off and place my hand over his and guide it, "All these feelings here in your belly and here in your chest, even here, in the back of your throat." I cradle his face in my hands so I can look him in the eyes for this, use my thumbs to clear his cheeks. "All these feelings are right. This is how your body reacts to seeing and doing this kind of thing because every part of you recognizes life and what it means to take it."

"What are we going to do with it now that it's all cut up like that?"

"Leave it for that eagle, or whatever else is around. That much blood will bring something."

✼

"Dad? Why did we have to just leave it? I thought we were supposed to save the fur."

He made it all the way back to the truck before asking. He's right; legally you have to salvage the pelt. Would've sold well, even.

"Wasn't ours."

"Then why —"

"Wasn't that asshole's kill, neither."

When we turn onto the Steese highway, my phone gets signal. Four alerts come in back-to-back. I toss Jacob the phone.

"It's Mom. Give her a call, let her know we're on our way."

He doesn't get much more past "Hi" before handing me the phone. There's something in Linda's voice that settles deep, sends all the muscles in my chest pulling against each other.

54

"Nathan? The hospital called. They're flying Whit to Anchorage. It's bad, Nate. You need to go."

❊

"I've packed you a bag and started checking flights. Do you think Jacob should go?"

"He's not going. Hell, I'm not going."

Linda's hair was pulled back in a ponytail and her hairline was damp from sweat. She'd been busy. Our little cabin is impeccable, and caustic from the cleaner fumes. It's what she does when she's worried. "Of course you're going. And Jacob's never met Whit. He should get that chance."

She's trying. I can see it, but I don't want to. I sit at the kitchen table and start idly poking through the bag she packed. Clothes, a camera, my knife, and my only suit. I pull out the knife, run my thumb down the blade. *Dull as dishwater* is what he would have called it. Never made sense to me, that saying. I get it, I guess, dishwater gets that dank gray, loses all the sparkle of fresh water. Sunny day on a river with a little chop to it and every little lap and break in the water will blind you, but you can't stop watching.

Linda pulls my hat off, slides her hand down the back of my head and between my coat and my neck. Not too much contact, just enough to count. "I'll go check on Jacob, see if I can get some of that blood out before it sets in."

I've still got the knife in my hands. Turning it over and over. The haft's made from a caribou antler. Whit made it for me. Well, the blade itself is some cheap knife Big Ray's was giving out as a promotion. He chiseled the plastic handle away and heated the tang with a little butane torch, the one he kept in the truck *just in case*. Got it red hot so it'd slide right through the antler. Better than drilling it; having the tang burnt in makes it tighter, like the bone moves itself out of the way to hold the blade. Like it wants it there. Of course it doesn't. Still, it looks nice. Even when it's stained rusty with blood.

It was sharp, once. Cut right into Dusty. I didn't mean it. But, *ain't no one ever gonna give two shits about what you mean, boy. What you do's all that means anything.* It was a Duke #330 beaver trap by the little pond out back. I never even saw a beaver out there, just liked the idea of it. Whit found my trap while out looking for Dusty. He'd known that a still-full food bowl was trouble. The trap got the dog's foreleg, right up above the carpal pad. He had thrashed against the steel until most of that little nub of meat tore free, but of course that didn't stop the trap from holding tight to the bone. Whit brought me out to see what I'd done, just left Dusty there until I could see him whimpering and licking. *Do it, boy.* The blood on the face from licking a wound, that must be why people think animals chew themselves free. Guess most only see the end, and sometimes there's no sense in looking for how you got there. *Fix what you did, son.*

I tried. Tried to get the trap off his leg. Dusty wouldn't let me. By then, all the dog had left his blue eyes. He was just animal. Tore into my sleeve when I reached for him. Whit let that happen, then grabbed hold of the animal, wrapped his cold-cracked hands around him like a muzzle. *Don't worry, little duct tape'll fix that. Not this, though. You know what to do. Start up under the jaw. Be quick. Anything else makes it worse.* And so I did it.

Whit took a knee beside me, eased the knife out of my hand. He dragged the flat of the blade across my forehead, down each cheek. *There ya go, first kill.* He dropped the knife beside me and walked away. *I'll get you the shovel.*

✿

"So, gutting a lynx and leaving it? That how Whit taught you?"
"Guess our little Jaybird told you about our day. You mad?"
"At you or the asshole?"
"Same difference."
Linda sets to scrubbing his parka with a bar of lye soap she keeps special just for blood. I never understood how that works. Having lye made to mix with water. But it works, so I guess the how isn't important.

I'm going to go. Don't know how to say it yet. Seems like the kind of thing that needs to have some gravity behind it, that's what decisions like these should feel like, right? I'm waiting to feel like I'm going to watch him die for some reason other than to watch him die.

"We both know you're going. You know Whit did what he thought he needed to. I'm not saying that makes him right, but after your mom —"

Linda drags one of the wooden chairs closer to mine, does that thing where she holds my forearm with both her hands so I know how to listen.

"Nathan, Jacob deserves to meet his grandfather."

But Jacob doesn't deserve that; he met him enough today. Already got all he taught me. What he taught me was about necessity, about being a man. Didn't teach me nothing about being a dad, because that's doing more than you need to.

"Just me. Jacob don't need to see him like that. Wait until after, maybe at the funeral. They'll make him peaceful."

❊

The flat stretch out past Summit Lake, that's my favorite part of the drive to Anchorage. So much nothing being exactly what it's supposed to be. It's above the tree line, so you just got that rocky scrub that burns purple when the fireweed blossoms. This time of year, at this elevation, it never really gets full-on dark, either. It gets close, but then twilight bleeds into dawn. Gives it a kind of blue glow, like an alcohol flame, but that little light will set the rest to burning if you give it a minute. And there's nothing but time out here. Time slathered across the hills and brush. It's the only time you'll ever get that goes on forever.

Then you hit Talkeetna, Houston, Willow, Wasilla, Eagle, Anchorage. All lined up. Seems like a sin, erasing all that time you just had.

❊

Looking into his room through the window, the old man looks even less than he is. Makes him seem more gray, transparent. He saw through me, too, that first day, before the third stroke. Now his eyes are the gray-blue of glacial water, and they loll around the way a caribou with a broken neck does when it's decided not to die.

He's not awake much, not going to be. The doctor tells me it was in the brainstem. Or at least the last one was. Tells me he'll never feed himself again, never breathe on his own again. Tells me it was something special to hang on this long.

The doctor talks about the feeding tube, says it's time to start thinking about options. About *comfort*. Because "pain" and "starvation" make it too primal. The old man's got so many tubes going in and out of him that he looks sewn to the room. And it's loud.

Synthetic loud. Gives it an oily, plastic texture. So, I ask the doctor to cut him loose. Get it all off of him, every damn tube. The doctor tells me it might not be quick, that there's nothing he can do about that.

When they come to do it, they won't let me stand by him. I watch from the corner as they go to work pulling him loose from the web holding him here. When they finally leave, I drag the chair up to the bed. I hold his hand, his skin still as cracked and calloused as it's always been. Cracked in the way the bottom of a dry riverbed cracks in the heat, broken by what it held and lost. His breaths blow ragged and dusty across his lips, rattling like wind through autumn leaves. The whole of him seems husk. So, I stay with him. Because I need to. I watch him die because we deserve that much.

SPECIAL SECTION: On Suicide

Content warning: Mention of suicide and discussions of mental health conditions and suicidal ideation. The following pages contain memoir, poetry, and thoughts dealing with the topic of suicide. If you are feeling vulnerable or unwell, please seek help. Perhaps put this little book down for now and reach out for support: Text HOME to 741741, the Crisis Text Line. **https://www.crisistextline.org**

National Suicide Prevention Lifeline: 1-800-273-8255 or dial 988

The International Association for Suicide Prevention has provided pre-written messages to help you reach out to people you trust. For example, you could use the following to contact someone: "When you get a chance can you contact me? I feel really alone and suicidal, and could use some support." **https://www.iasp.info/suicidalthoughts/**

HoldOn2Hope Project: A project to "unite creatives in mental health awareness and suicide prevention." **https://www.holdon2hope.org/**

The Society of Authors and Samaritans have a downloadable guide: *Depiction of suicide and self-harm in literature.* **https://societyofauthors. org/SOA/MediaLibrary/SOAWebsite/Documents-for-download/ Samaritans-Suicide_and_self_harm_Literature_.pdf**

INTRODUCTION

When we first read the essay that follows, Andrew Stevens's "Punch Card," we were struck by his literary craft: his use of structure and the unique collection of reasons to keep living—from the punch card to his dear ones. We accepted the piece and worked with Andrew to polish it. Then one of our editors pointed out the obvious: that we were reading the voice of a person who was considering suicide. Concerned, we consulted mental health professionals, who recommended that we check in with Andrew to make sure he was all right. We did, and he was. He let us know that he had good support.

We were greatly relieved. Then we did some thinking. Andrew's forthright exploration of this subject brought candor—and a perspective we don't often hear—to an important issue. We researched the ethics of publishing this material. And we decided to try something new.

Part of publishing, for us, is holding things in the light—bringing attention, through words, to things of beauty or importance. We decided to publish Andrew's piece nested within supporting material: We asked Andrew to write about his intentions. We reached out to Detroit area poet Linda Sienkiewicz, who recently published *Sleepwalker* (Finishing Line Press), a beautiful chapbook of poetry that responds to the loss of her son to suicide, and asked for her reflections. We reached out to Judy Chu for her essay on losing a student. And Dean Engle sent us an essay that fit into this section.

When we discovered the work of Grand Rapids area artist Ann Willey, we were drawn to "Off the Path," the painting that adorns the cover. We hope that this mini-collection of pieces will shine a bit of light on the intricate feelings of people who are facing great pain—either the pain of living or the pain of losing a loved one.

Andrew Stevens
PUNCH CARD

There is a punch card in my pocket with ten fish-shaped punches in it. My preferred fast-casual Tex-Mex semi-local chain restaurant hasn't finished switching over to the deliberately confusing digital point-based system, so they've still got me on analog punch cards until it's ready.

They're known for their fish tacos, but I've never had one. I am a man of routine. A ground beef burrito on a green spinach tortilla with pico de gallo, lettuce, hot salsa, no beans, and extra rice. Both sour cream and guacamole. I don't even say my order out loud anymore. The same kind Indian man makes small talk with me about the weather as he wraps my lunch. I go in every Monday for double punches and usually once again later in the week.

That's why I can't do it. I can't break my routine.

There are two pills of Depakote and three pills of lithium tumbling down my throat. I scoop water from the sink with a cupped hand and toss it into my mouth like I'm a YouTube prankster throwing a clump of flour in the face of a passerby. I clumsily try to swallow the pills and fail and gag and choke on the flavor and the texture as they teeter on the back of my tongue. I repeat the water-tossing process to get them down.

They aren't working.

I've given lithium nine months of my life and all I've gotten is dehydrated. My psychiatrist always has more ideas. He doesn't like me saying "treatment-resistant." Not yet. Even after an ensemble cast of medications: Celexa, Lexapro, Effexor, Abilify, Vraylar, Wellbutrin, Gabapentin, antidepressants, mood stabilizers, antipsychotics, beta-blockers, benzodiazepines, and the rest.

My last psychiatrist would ask me, "What are you looking forward to?" at the end of every session. When I speak to my current therapist and she asks me the same question, I wonder if I see a bit of panic in her eyes that she's trying to hide. I think she fears what it might mean if I didn't show up for my next session.

I mention weddings and birthday parties, concerts I already bought tickets to, whatever trips I've planned. But mostly, I rarely look forward to the next day, especially when each one is so similar to the day prior, as it has been now for years.

She casually brings up hospitalization from time to time with light concern in her voice. I remind her that would put my job and my cat at risk.

That's why I can't do it. I have to take care of my cat.

Yet I am currently caving in.

My lows are low. Filthy water in the eye of the drain. My highs are low, too. Some bipolar people get irritable instead of euphoric; that's why the diagnosis took so long. Ten years of taking the wrong drugs for the wrong disorder. Who knew? Seems like I should have.

I've sobbed in front of everyone at the bar more than any man I've ever known – how did I not know I was bipolar?

I'm embarrassed at my own shortsightedness. Ashamed of all the times I thought I was smart when I was really self-righteous. Hypomania is a puppeteer, steering my strings toward self-aggrandizing statements and an ersatz sense of superiority. Depression is an autonomous pair of pliers that twists every memory into something that makes me wince. Everything I've said and done – and even the things people say I've done that I haven't – compounds to critical mass.

My body and brain are failing on me. I am falling apart quite literally from head to toe. From the itchy eczema on my scalp, which leaves crusted blood beneath my manicured nails when I scratch, to my inexplicably swollen feet that elicited one "Wow" too many from my podiatrist when he gave them an ultrasound. I shouldn't be in this sort of shape in my early thirties, but my semi-sedentary lifestyle was made exponentially worse by the world transformed – nay, revealed – by the pandemic.

I buy salicylic acid for my head and compression socks for my feet. I take more pills to get the swelling down. I'm taking eleven pills a day to fix everything that's wrong. Yet still I remain thoroughly unfixed. Hope seems abstract and unreal, although some small part of me clings to it.

That's why I can't do it. In case I can make things like they used to be.

But time rambles forward and years have been lost; while others seem to progress, I stutter and stagnate. I succumb to the darkness of my thoughts – a black pit of piranhas, each razor-sharp tricuspid another regret, swimming circles in a warm stew of liquid shame.

I am both lonely and alone much of the time.

I read an article about the loneliness epidemic that says loneliness raises the risk of premature death, and I fantasize about my own aneurysm. It wouldn't hurt other people as much if I didn't do it myself. No one would repeat that false mantra: "I wish we could have done something."

That's why I can't do it. I don't want to hurt anyone else. Just myself.

I won't let down my cat and my mom, though I know my cat would find a new home with ease on account of that adorable face he has. But my mom might never recover; my father's infidelity and their subsequent divorce led to three separate mental breakdowns and hospitalizations. I don't know what losing me would do to her. She'd still have one son left, but I don't think that'd ease the pain any. I can't put her through it, no matter how miserable it may be for me to stick around.

But eventually both my mom and my cat are going to be gone too.

As I rack my brain for reasons to stay, I think of which of my friends is next to get married, and I remind myself of how my empty seat at their wedding will cause them pain.

Though I'm always secretly a little sour at witnessing a culmination of love that I will never find myself, I still find nothing more important than showing up to celebrate the unions of the people I care about the most.

That's why I can't do it. I've got three weddings this year, and I see more engagements on the horizon.

I read over and over about the celebrities who did it and I think about all the people they influenced, their families, the outpouring of love and support they had, all their money and wealth and power, the sense of accomplishment, the admiration of their peers, and how none of it was enough to keep them around.
What chance could I possibly have with those odds? What strength could I have that Robin Williams or Chris Cornell didn't?
I take a bong rip on my broken couch after work, and I scroll through films and TV shows on my many streaming services, searching for something distracting to help me pass the time. The red voice that wakes me every morning tells me I'm worthless and that I have nothing left to offer anyone, and I can't find the blue voice that ever-so-slightly disagrees until I fill my lungs with smoke.
I like stupid superhero movies: they're always announcing the next one. Which gives me something to look forward to.

That's why I can't do it. There's a new Thor *movie coming out.*

The weekend comes and goes and I quietly weep in the back of a Lyft while I write my suicide note on my phone, my fingers trembling as I try to get the words that have raced through my head for months onto the page.

I reread the note every day, knowing it is not a matter of *if*, but when. Sometimes I hope I will find the courage soon, and other times I hope I can hold out for at least another year.

When you drift downward into the deepest trenches of despair, you must search for the air that keeps you from drowning: people or pets or events or movies or anything else you can grasp onto.

And so I *can't* do it. Not yet.

Because then I won't get my free burrito. And I've got ten punches on my punch card: I earned that fucking thing.

Interview with Andrew Stevens
ON WRITING *PUNCH CARD*

Editors: We asked Andrew Stevens to share his thoughts on his creative nonfiction essay "Punch Card."

Dunes Review: **To begin, here's a general question that writers are often asked: What were your intentions for this piece? What were you thinking about and how did you come to shape it the way you did?**

Andrew Stevens: When I started, it was my lowest point ever. My therapist told me repeatedly to write out my feelings. Finally, I did, just as a way to get thoughts onto paper. I first wrote about my feelings, not reasons to stay alive. Gradually, it became a method of convincing myself there were reasons to stay. Anything that popped into my head, I used for the structure, starting with the first stupid, tiny thing where I'd thought "Not yet"—wanting my free burrito. And I kept going.

Eventually, I realized this exercise had captured an important, horrible moment in my life. My worst moments are my biggest inspirations: my broken family, volatile relationships, self-hatred, addiction, trauma. But I'd never written about active suicidal ideation. I had my plan, gathered supplies, knew where I'd do it, wrote my note. The only thing keeping me alive was not committing to when. And ultimately, telling this to my psychiatrist and switching medications.

My last published piece was about passive suicidal ideation; I once read it at an open mic. Someone said to me afterward, "Thank you. You get it." Remembering that, I had to finish this piece: both to help people like me be seen and to articulate my feelings to my loved ones.

DR: **We selected this piece because of the literary imagination and skill you brought to this topic. At the same time, it seems important to acknowledge that suicide or suicidal ideation is a topic about which we could all learn something. What would you like readers to be curious about or to understand?**

AS: What I'd want people to understand is that even with therapy and medication, this doesn't go away. Depression and bipolar disorder aren't defeated, only managed. How I felt when I began writing this is how many others feel. I wanted to emphasize finding anything that gets them to say "Not yet." If you know someone with depression, they may also be searching for reasons to live.

The best book I've read on depression is Andrew Solomon's *The Noonday Demon*. One repeated question he received came from people with depressed loved ones: "How can I help?" His answer: "Blunt their isolation. Do it with cups of tea or with long talks or by sitting in a room nearby and staying silent or in whatever way suits the circumstances, but do that. And do it willingly." Another quote comes from someone he interviewed: "Whoever loves me, loves me with this in it."

I have one more quote from Andrew Solomon's *The Noonday Demon* in terms of what people should understand about suicide.

"Contrary to popular belief, suicide is not the last resort of the depressive mind. It is not the last moment of mental decay. The chances of suicide are actually higher among people returned from a hospital stay than they are among people at a hospital, and not simply because the restraints of the hospital setting have been lifted. Suicide is the mind's rebellion against itself, a double disillusionment of a complexity that the perfectly depressed mind cannot compass. It is a willful act to liberate oneself of oneself. The meekness of depression could hardly imagine suicide; it takes the brilliance of self-recognition to destroy the object of that recognition. However misguided the impulse, it is at least an impulse. If there is no other comfort in a suicide not avoided, at least there is this persistent thought, that it was an act of misplaced courage and unfortunate strength rather than an act of utter weakness or of cowardice."

DR: **Is there anything else you'd like us to know about this piece?**

AS: I'd just want to mention where I wound up afterwards. It took an extremely unpleasant year-plus of trial and error, trying to find the right treatment. It wound up being an ancient, last-ditch-effort antidepressant, and I haven't had an extreme bout of depression in seven months. With another medication I began taking a few months ago, I was able to crank down parts of my hypomania as well. I'm better than I was, but like I said, these feelings will never be entirely gone.

I'm notoriously an open, honest person, to a fault. But I only talked to a few friends about what I was going through when I wrote this. The topic felt like a taboo I couldn't easily discuss. I wrote this to talk about the one thing I didn't know how to say to people, and also so others who relate might find an iota of inspiration in it that helps them stick around, too.

Linda Sienkiewicz
THE SECOND WORST THING

on the day
we found you
the police made us leave

your apartment
Crime scene, they said

though it wasn't

your father and I sat
on the hard rubber treads
of the stairs in the hallway

the landlady fretted

I made a phone call
or two

the police took
your laptop
your notebooks

I don't know what else—

and then
you

The next worst thing—
your aunt running
down the sidewalk
arms waving
screaming

and later
your eighty-nine year-old
grandmother
crying
in my lap

Linda Sienkiewicz
AFTER TEN YEARS MY LATE SON VISITS

He parks his Hummer in the driveway,
comes in the back door.
How's it goin', Moms?

I say, *As well as can be.*
You know.

He says, *I know.*

I say, *Do you miss me?*

He says he misses
his Egyptian cotton sheets.

I offer him pot roast,
his favorite.

He says he quit eating.
Just gave it up.

I ask if he's cold.
He looks cold,
too thin. *I worry*
about you.
What's it like?
Are you still sad?

He says, *You don't have to*
worry anymore.

I say, *I can't stop. A mother just can't.*
I wish I would have told you
that. There are so many things
I wish I would have told you.

He says, *You can tell me*
now. I'll listen.

Linda Sienkiewicz
SOLO SUITE

Linden's cello sighs
with each bow stroke
across the gut strings,
Solo Suite Number Three
in C major.
His head drops,
his eyes close,
his hand dances.
The cello weeps,
sighs, trills
and moans.

I hear you
in the sad
unhurried
depths.
Transported
from the audience
to sudden witness
in another time,
I see your hand
suspended
in the air
above your chest,
fingers frozen,
eyes closed,
your throat
tightly wrapped,
imagine your
last breath
in the final sigh

before you asked
death to take you.
I wanted

to push
your arm down,
beg please,
tell me, son,
what I see
isn't so,
what I hear
isn't
my own weeping.

Interview with Linda Sienkiewicz

Editors: We asked poet Linda Sienkiewicz a few of the same questions we posed to Andrew Stevens, to contextualize the connections between their work and provide a framework for reflection and discussion among readers.

Dunes Review: **To begin, here's a general question that writers are often asked: What were your intentions for these pieces? What were you thinking about and how did you come to shape them the way that you did?**

Linda Sienkiewicz: My son took his own life in 2011. About three years after his death, I wrote an essay about the black hill spruce tree we got for our first Christmas without him. Beyond that, I never had any intention to write poems about him or his suicide. Rather, I actively avoided it because it the pain was too much to bear. Then, in 2019, I attended a performance with friends to see a Dutch cellist, Jaap ter Linden. One of his songs, "Solo Suite," was so sad and haunting that it took me back to the moment when my husband and I had found our son, deceased, in his apartment. There, at the concert, the start of a poem came to me while I fought tears. When I returned home, I felt compelled to write a poem addressing my son directly. That poem, "Solo Suite," was later a Finalist for the 2022 Julia Darling Poetry Prize.

Writing about him, and, in particular, writing poems as if speaking to him, was like doing a deep dive into an emotional maelstrom. Even working on the draft of "Solo Suite" made me cry. I had trouble sleeping. I had sad dreams. I had to allow myself to walk away from it. It didn't feel cathartic until much later. I found solace in the small cemetery in my neighborhood. When I read the gravestones of babies, children and young adults who are buried next to their parents, I realized I was not alone in my grief. Illness, accidents and suicide take lives of loved ones every single day. It's not fair, but it is reality. Life is fragile. The hope that my poetry could help to others who have suffered the loss of a loved one to suicide kept me motivated to keep writing. We need to be able to talk openly about suicide, grief and loss.

DR: **We selected these pieces because of the literary imagination and skill you brought to this topic. At the same time, it seems important to acknowledge that suicide or suicidal ideation is a topic about which we could all learn something. What would you like readers to be curious about or to understand?**

LS: Suicide is difficult because of the stigma. People will ask "How did this happen?" or "Weren't there signs?" and then you begin to wonder, *did I do everything I could have to prevent this?* Unfortunately you'll never know. We had taken our son to the hospital before, and we were about to do so again, but we were about 12 hours too late. If we had reached him in time, he might have gotten better, but who's to say he wouldn't have stopped taking medication again? You can't force an adult to take antidepressants. You can't force them into therapy. That aspect breaks my heart.

It won't always hurt. One day you will be able to talk about your loved one and the loss without crying. You will feel joy and happiness again, and you will accept that it's all right to feel joy and happiness. We honor our son in little ways. On his birthday, we get pepperoni pizza because it was his favorite. Every Christmas, we decorate a small tree with the ornaments I collected for him since he was a baby. We keep his picture out. We talk about him, "Oh, Derek would have loved this," or "Remember the first time we took him to the beach?" It's important to share good memories.

Judy Y. Chu
AFTER PAUL KLEE:
IN MEMORY OF DREW KOSTIC

The print is abstract: no meal on a table, no beautiful landscape, no portrait of humanity, no moment of desperate conflict. Instead, just squares of color. Vibrant... no... muted yet somehow singing out in the center, framed by shadowy squares of drab beige, dull sage, muddy brown, seeping into black.

I see the shadowy black squares and think of graves; I see the colored tiles framed within, a wobbly grid, and think of lives lived in imperfect houses, farms and fields comprising a patchwork quilt. It looks like some stretches of countryside beyond my city's limits in northern Michigan, where many of my students live, driving in to attend the community college where I teach.

Beyond color, texture emerges with further scrutiny: brushstrokes visible in the lighter, lively hues that disappear into the darkened, shadowy edges.

*

December 2016, finals week: I am trying to grasp what the college Dean is telling me on my office phone, where I sit grading a stack of essays from my composition classes.

"Drew Kostic is dead."

I don't comprehend.

"He committed suicide this past weekend."

But he can't be dead, I think feebly. I have not yet started on his section's final project, a self-reflective essay of student growth as writer and thinker. The rest of the Dean's words trail off in my memory. Tears rush down my face. I strangle a cry into the cold gray phone receiver.

After filing final course grades, I go to Drew's memorial service, my first military funeral, on a hard, gray day before Christmas. Drew is not merely the first student in two decades of teaching I have lost to suicide, which is tragedy enough; he was also a non-traditional college student, a 28-year-old Marine veteran with three combat tours under his belt, who expertly concealed the struggles of his transition back to civilian life from everyone: his family, friends, and neighbors; his fellow veterans, classmates, and teachers; and ultimately himself.

I sit through patriotic country music blaring from speakers in a room crowded with family and friends and young men who look haunted, having come from across the country to pay respects to another one fallen from their ranks. I listen to his uncle, a colonel, saying we are there to honor Drew, that we don't need to dwell on the particular circumstances of his death. I shake his wife's hand, his high school sweetheart, a striking blonde clad in black. When I walk past the casket to pay my respects, I nod slightly at his father, a former Marine himself, who sits near the end of the front row, face ashen, shoulders bent, clutching a folded flag in his lap.

A month later, at the start of a new semester, I compartmentalize myself efficiently to cope with it all: my family's life, which goes on; my teaching, which goes on; the fractured body politic during a contentious presidential election, which goes on. To maintain my balance, what else do I seal off? Something quiet, buried within that I don't touch, until May, when the academic year ends, and I find myself at a Catholic retreat center on the edges of Santa Fe, sitting in a circle of strangers, surprised by morning snowfall in the high desert, sitting in Buddhist silence, sitting and writing, reading and listening for days, creeping slowly towards the pain that I had buried deep within.

To be sure, I thought about Drew through the months following his funeral, as we slogged our way through another northern Michigan winter and saw the return of crocuses along edges of yards and against back-alley fences. But as Drew's uncle the colonel advised, I resolved not to let myself dwell on the particular circumstances of my student's death, even though those words had sparked an anger in me during the funeral service. "He went out on his own terms," eulogized his uncle, which only made me seethe: *Why turn a soldier's death by his own hand into something heroic?* For me to get through my own life at that point, I couldn't think about the end of Drew's life. Grief is odd like that. The initial shock from the Dean's news on the phone, followed by the pain, anger, and loss felt at the funeral, gave way to a helpful numbness that saw me through the spring semester, convincing me somehow that I had my hand on the wheel, driving through my existence in Traverse City. So in May, as I flew out to Santa Fe, finally at a safe distance from my own life, from the semester, from polarizing presidential election results and Drew's funeral, only then was I able to reflect upon the tragedy of his suicide, and ask the question that must cross every teacher's mind when they wonder if they might have seen the signs, done something.

※

The Swiss-born German modernist Paul Klee was known for his surrealism, Cubism, and expressionism. As World War I was breaking out, according to Sabine Rewald, writing for the Metropolitan Museum of Art, he "gradually detached color from physical description and used it independently, which gave him the final needed push toward abstraction." From that point on in his career, configurations of colored rectangles or squares became a staple in his composition, "quilts of color, which he orchestrated into fantastic and childlike yet deeply meditative works".

Is it this quilt of color that draws me to Klee and invites my meditation?

❋

I didn't go out to Santa Fe seeking healing through Buddhist enlightenment in a Catholic setting. Instead, I had gone to a memoir workshop, and the locale also happened to house Carmelite nuns committed to a vow of silence, and the writing instructors happened to practice Buddhist meditation. What I hadn't counted on was how all that silence would beget writing would beget tears, and then more silence, more words on pages, more tears again.

On the third day, after sitting in silence and then writing, my workshop teachers said we could write down the names of those who had passed on and put the pieces of folded up paper on the Buddhist altar. I did so, and then cried. On the fourth day, after sitting in silence, I wrote about Drew and read my piece aloud in class, my eyes filling as I read the final sentences. (Afterwards, a former teacher told me about her student who had committed suicide, too.) After my week in Santa Fe ended, I was back home in Traverse City, at church for Memorial Day, when the pastor said we could write the name of a veteran we had known who was gone and place it under the uniform that a retired Marine Corps Lt. Colonel church member had hung up to help our congregation observe the day. After service, I burst out in tears to the Lt. Colonel's wife, herself a former Marine captain, telling her about my student's suicide. She was the first person to say to me, "I'm sorry for your loss," acknowledging that teachers are left bereft, too.

I sat and cried at home that summer, reading the latest *New York Times* analysis of continued American military operations in Iraq. I sat and cried and journaled daily, not always about Drew: more often about my childhood, my parents, my family's immigration stories; my 99-year-old friend, a WWII Navy Reserve WAVE we visited in the nursing home; my mother who suffers from depression and lives across the country; my own depression, which ebbs and flows—and just once had nudged me close enough to the edge to wonder if I could no longer bear to go on. I sat in silence and filled pages of notebooks those months, the tears finally coming less frequently, trying to write my way out of my grief.

Out? Can a teacher really write his or her way out of the suicide death of an exemplary student? Can a comfortably middle-class, middle-aged civilian female community college instructor, liberal in political viewpoint, write her way out of the self-inflicted death by gunshot wound of her student, a Marine combat vet, who showed up in her classes for two semesters, worked hard through her assignments, grew as a writer, and in his year-long stint in higher education, made the Dean's list both semesters—posthumously noted, the second time? Or if she can't write her way out of grief, can she write her way into some sort of understanding?

I am reminded that many use religion as a way of making meaning out of death, which offers comfort in some greater plan beyond human understanding. But even though I was raised in one faith tradition as a child, and continued in another as an adult, I didn't pray to my God when Drew died: for myself, for him, for his family. Instead, I sat. I cried. And I wrote.

Of course, words scratched in a journal are therapeutic, but I was hoping for something beyond just my own catharsis. I was trying to figure out something about Drew, someone I didn't really know. So I'd imagine and empathize. In the pages I wrote that summer after his death, I'd imagine what his father felt, what his wife felt, what his dog felt, even what that colonel uncle felt. I argued in my notebook with the politicians whose policies had deployed Drew. I argued with myself about what I should have noticed more, as his English teacher, meeting twice a week through two academic semesters. Throughout that summer, when I was often inconsolable (my husband and child tiptoed around the house those mornings I sat in the front room, writing and crying), I don't recall praying in the ways I had learned as a child or practiced as an adult.

Or maybe I did pray, about Drew and even in the end about me—because of course, my grief over Drew's suicide led me to recognize that sometimes, depression consumes: his ultimately did; mine thankfully didn't. There, but for the grace of God, go I. Maybe prayer exists in tears and words on notebook paper, a person groping for meaning with marks on page—or lines, squares, colors, and shadows on canvas. And maybe some healing can emerge there, too.

*

According to a 2014 report by the U.S. Department of Veteran Affairs, twenty veterans commit suicide per day, with the number spiking among those ages 18 to 29. Twenty per day. While most of those suicides are by older veterans, I still wonder how many are Drew's age, no longer the kid who enlisted, but someone older and changed. How many come back from their time in the military, looking for a place, role, or purpose in civilian society—thinking college might be a pathway? How many take a seat in a classroom like mine, while feeling like an alien on campus? How many show up or disappear from our classes?

In 2018, two years after that Fall semester when the world was imploding around Drew, I stumble across Paul Klee's painting in another writing workshop, this time in the Hudson River Valley, prompted by another instructor to pick a painting from among a table covered with print copies of different works of art. Ekphrasis, she explains, a new concept to me: We would study the painting, follow her questions, and write in response.

So I sit, staring at the colored squares, surrounded by shadow. I start to write about a patchwork grid of houses, farm fields, and graves in the midwestern place I call home—and somehow, I am back in the countryside where I imagine Drew once lived.

I am surprised when I learn the title of Klee's 1925 painting, "Abstraction with Reference to a Flowering Tree," because where I saw dark squares gravely marking out the border, the title suggests that the artist actually worked to harmonize the shimmering vibrancy of leaves on a tree. A study in color, in life, in song, it turns out: a flowering tree transformed into colorful, rippled, geometric abstraction. I had focused on the shadows, drawn by the darkness setting off all that color and light. Yet according to a review of a Klee exhibit by Alana Shilling-Janoff in The Brooklyn Rail, a journal focused on the arts, politics, and culture, "The experience of viewing Klee's work should be joyful."

Still, darkness looms out there, swirling at the edges, sometimes engulfing. After dissolving the Bauhaus School, on whose faculty Klee had served during the 1920s, the Nazis classified the artist's work as "filth": seventeen of his paintings were included in their 1937 exhibition of "Degenerate Art." Klee died of scleroderma, an autoimmune wasting disease, in Switzerland, the summer of 1940.

❋

In a way, the problem was—is—one of perception. Teachers and students exist in the delicate classroom ecosystem that both parties imagine they might have some control over. Sometimes we do. Yet often, we don't. As Drew's teacher, I could note how he used earphones to drown out the noise of the room, before class began, but I couldn't see or hear what he was trying to block out. If in the end he could only focus on his own suffering, then he couldn't see the part of himself struggling to be well.

The swirling darkness proved too much for Drew, after he returned to civilian life and tried to make sense of, move on from, his combat experience. It was too difficult, ultimately impossible, for him to see for himself a life back in northern Michigan, even as others around him were trying to help him see that life and pathway forward. And this is what hurts: that gaps in perception silenced his story. I am left wondering now, as I contemplate Klee's invitation: How to allow for both shadows and color? How to see—and live with—both?

Dean Engle
ONE OF NINE

A red fox stands in a field of white snow, its paws sinking into the drift, its fur matted with melting flakes. The fox leans its head to one side, ears perking up. It is still for a moment, and then dashes across the snow, leaving only its delicate prints. In the distance a gunshot rings out and echoes into an unbroken silence.

Adults have a voice for telling secrets they don't want you to hear. It is a hushed voice, but never quite a whisper. A voice that doesn't want to be picked up by the wind, tossed about wildly to the wrong set of ears. The tone lowers, to signify importance, to signify the words have weight.

So, when I heard my aunt use this voice, barely audible from the next room, I had to listen. It was not polite, I knew. But the house was small and I was curious. She was on the phone with her boyfriend. This is what I heard her say.

"You know my brother Jim, the one who killed himself."

And there I had an answer to something I'd always wondered. My mother, whenever talking about her family, used the same phrase, rote at this point. "I'm one of nine." One of nine. Not so unusual for the time—our family was Irish Catholic, after all. What was unusual was the numbering. I only ever counted eight. Gathered for pictures at family barbeques or hovering around the drink table at Christmas parties the equation was always the same. One mother, two uncles, five aunts. One of eight.

But at the same time, I had heard of Jim. Usually in that same voice, hushed and heavy. Just a little something here or there, nothing very interesting.

"Is that Jim's China?"

"Do you remember Jim's old motorcycle?"

"I spilled ice-cream everywhere. I could see Jim trying to stay calm."

Little things about this man, my uncle, that never spun together into a clear picture. None of these were ever said around my grandmother. And there were no pictures of him in her home, though there was a picture of everyone else. Of every other child and grandchild. In mine, I am so young I'm still blonde, holding a rake next to an oversized pile of leaves. Around the frame, animals dance in the snow: a reindeer, a polar bear, and a fox.

But now, my aunt had revealed the reason the numbering was off. I suppose I had known Jim was dead. If he had been alive, there would have been more to say.

I listened closer to the door, but I did not hear any more. Jim had been brought up again, only in passing. My aunt had wanted to know his rank. Her conversation drifted elsewhere, and I returned to my silent room.

I sat on this, for a day or two, not wanting to tell my aunt I had been spying. But needing to know more. I finally asked my mother point-blank about her brother.

She remembered Jim as the most protective of her siblings, the one most ready to stick up for the younger ones, the one most willing to take them on a joy ride, even when she spilled ice cream in the back seat. The ice cream: another piece fell into place.

Jim had been in the Navy. He had been stationed in Japan and met a woman. They got married and were going to have a child. They lost the child before it was born. My mother told these facts to me, in a somewhat distant tone. She was not cold about it, not uncaring. Instead, she was trying to understand something from many years ago.

"We got one last letter from him," she told me. "He was holding a fox in the snow." In the end, he hanged himself from a phone line. I can picture it clearly, boot prints leading to the pole, other than that the snow untouched.

My grandmother arranged for his body to be sent back home, but never spoke of it. Suicide was a sin. So, if it came up, she said it was an accident, far away. She and Jim's wife exchanged a few letters, though they were not with my grandmother's correspondences when she died. They are buried together, my two grandparents and their son, in a Catholic cemetery. My grandmother must have lied about the cause of death.

It is hard to gain a full idea of my uncle through these scatterings of half-remembered facts and half-forgotten memories. But I can see him for a moment.

Jim, russet hair and golden eyes, trudging through a frostbitten field, huge boot prints next to the hint of paws. A gun is slung over one shoulder as he walks toward the body. He will take the carcass, snap a picture, and send it home enclosed in an envelope. But still I pray, though I am no longer Catholic, that the body will twitch, the ears will perk up, and the fox will rise and sprint off into the forest, out of the snow.

René Ostberg
DREAM PACZKI

Day one ends in plain exhaustion, day two in a frenetic dream. As if having the smell of them all over me or their crumbs lodged beneath my fingernails isn't enough, I have to see them in my sleep. Before sleep, even, just by sitting down during a shift break and closing my eyes. Moving relentlessly behind my eyelids like newspapers on a conveyor belt in an old-time movie montage. Hands grabbing at them to put them in boxes and more boxes. Hands nicked with papercuts, and red and chapped from constant washing. The phone rings nonstop for orders we can barely keep up with, the register rings for purchases, the receipt roll at the shift changeover runs a mile long. At night it takes ages to stop hearing echoes, the voices of customers and my co-workers calling numbers, rattling off flavors. I dream paczki. And each morning I feel as if I'm waking to the eerie silence before a tornado's touchdown.

Mid-pandemic I took a side job, a clerk in the storefront of a local bakery. It was only part-time, but it felt as familiar as something you do all the time. Me and the work went way back to when I was twenty years old and taking cooking classes at a community college, paying every cent of my tuition with my minimum-wage earnings.

Like most essential workers—something nobody thought to designate us retail and bakery grunts back then—I worked weekends and holidays, up with the chickens even on mornings when I'd been out all night. At twenty, I still kept hours like that, could handle being on my feet, running back and forth from register to customer, carrying heavy cakes, making it through a shift on just a few minutes' break or a few winks of sleep.

Right away I discovered food service work was nothing like it was portrayed on shows like *Friends*, or in a culinary culture increasingly oriented toward the "foodie," a still-newish word not so liberally used back then. Media chefs seemed to get their pick of days off, got to travel the world, enjoy fame and fortune, rub shoulders with rock stars, were considered rock stars themselves. It was a world away from my community college cooking classes and bakery job. In the real world, food workers are chained to weekends and holidays. Thanksgiving, Christmas, Easter, graduations and First Communions, Mother's Day, June weddings, Memorial Day picnics—all occasions that kept us on the run from fall through spring.

But our busiest time of year was pre-Lent, when the bakery sold paczki: Polish donuts filled with fruit, cream, or mousse, then glazed or dusted with powdered sugar to rich perfection. Where I live, just outside Chicago, a mecca for generations of Polish immigrants, people live for the paczki. In the week leading up to Ash Wednesday, customers told us so more than a baker's dozen times a day. They'd even stand in line for hours, enduring the wait for something that came around only once a year. The entire week, we workers never stopped running, with production ramped up to the fastest we could go.

Paczki time was as festive as it was frenzied. Something of a party, with the desperate feel of last calls or last chances. As the saying goes, "Eat, drink, and be merry, for tomorrow we may die." One worker would dress up as a giant paczki and pass out samples. We'd wear Mardi Gras beads, hang banners with bright colors and cartoon donuts across the storefront windows. Customers would occasionally break out in cheers when their ticket number was called. A local news crew might show up. The reporter would weave through the crowd, ask each customer their favorite flavor, how long they'd been waiting, and was it worth it? (Strawberries and whip cream, over an hour, and oh yes. Yesiree.)

Nothing about it was meant to be ironic. In the working-class heartland, food is far too complex for irony. Food is fuel, comfort, love. A family bond, through handed-down recipes or inherited eating habits. An occasion for wholesome fun, like Christmas cookie exchanges, or for heartfelt compassion, like a neighbor's dish of funeral potatoes. Paczki, invented to use up all the fat and sugar in the cupboard before the religious fasting season begins, bear the additional weight of Catholic guilt and the sinfulness of waste. And for bakery grunts, they bear the weight of labor.

To call something "essential" is to suggest it's eternal. Trends come and go, technology changes, but our needs and the labor and actions we undertake to satisfy them are universal and constant.

Without the essential, time would stop. Life for all would end. Eat, drink, and be merry, for real.

As for essential workers, we know we're essential, that the world depends on us for sustenance, for healing, for clothes, and for our daily bread. But it's the difference between knowing it and feeling it that essential workers have to reckon with when they punch out. It's the difference between a new term that gets tossed around in headlines and the day-to-day treatment you're given on the job.

Back at the bakery, thirty years on, sometimes I felt essential. Needed. Appreciated. But most times I felt like a human treadmill, a mere vehicle for a force beyond my control.

Donning my work apron seemed like old times, and yet so much had changed. An online shop took a load off the madness of phone and in-store orders. The register's punch buttons were now a computerized touchscreen, with excruciatingly small print for my fifty-year-old eyes. The variety of paczki had expanded to a menu of thirty-plus flavors, from red velvet to "Elvis" (bananas with maple custard and bacon). Faves were counted by numbers sold and TikTok polls.

The other stuff wasn't selling as well — bread, coffee cakes, muffins, or regular ol' donuts. Not with offices closed, remote work in full force, and funerals banned or kept to private services with the bare minimum of mourners. We were perpetually short-staffed. No one wants to face crowds during a pandemic. No one wants to wear masks for hours of a shift. No one wants to risk their life for retail — not for under fifteen dollars an hour. No one but the grunts, the essential.

The day before Ash Wednesday, the last call for paczki, my state lifted its masks in public mandate. We workers kept ours on at all times, but you could see relief in the eyes and smiles of customers who went maskless as they stood in line for paczki. Still, my fellow grunts noted how strangely quiet the crowd was, almost like a herd of sleeping cows, none of the *"laissez les bon temps rouler"* of years past, long before the pandemic. Maybe it was that difference between knowing and feeling again. Was the pandemic really over? Could we truly breathe easy again? Would things go back to normal or go on to a kinder, fairer society? Which one were we supposed to want? Productivity, after all, is a hard drug to wean yourself from, no matter how happy you are to see the system take a hit, how long you've been dreaming to step off the treadmill, to throw a wrench in it yourself.

Many years ago, when the wife of a world-famous rock star died, a story went around about how he nurtured her through her last moments with a whispered memory vision of her favorite things. Her horse. Spring weather. Woods. Bluebells. A blue sky. During the lockdown days of the pandemic, I thought about that story more than once. In a time of daily mass death counts, maybe it simply struck me as the model of a good end.

It didn't take Covid-19 or a job as an essential worker to learn I don't want to work myself to death. That I don't want my life to come down to filling orders, fearing crowds, washing my hands to rawness, running my feet off, worrying myself to sleep, dreaming an assembly line of paczki. Hoping for a better life is instinctual, essential, and that kind of thing originates in the heart and soul long before anyone learns about capitalism, productivity, irony, foodieism, or rock star treatment.

Eat, drink, and be merry. Tomorrow may be better.

Bee LB
ODE TO THE HUNGRY
after Susan Nguyen

praise WIC and each shelf labeled for a mother's need
to cure hunger. praise the lifelong cure.

praise the formula kept on open shelves
and the mothers who steal it.
abandon the store's lock guard and key.

praise food stamps, bridge cards, hungry mouths
and crowded homes. abandon the assistance application form

the yearly updates, the exact number in a bank account.
abandon the assets listing. abandon the proof of need.

trust and praise the open mouths, waiting hands, empty bellies.

abandon the waste of excess. riot against the borders of hunger.
demolish the demonstration of power as police guard the food-filled dumpsters.

praise the theft of food named waste.

praise the theft of profit from those who have never known hunger
without its imminent end.

praise the food pantries, community kitchens,
the dumpster-diving redistributors. praise the hungry.

praise the hungry. praise the hungry. praise the pleasure
found in the first meal you learn to cook for yourself.

praise the microwave and its gift of ease. praise the sweet crisp of fresh vegetables.
praise the drive-thru's 2-for-1 deal and the credit card's 5% cash back
and abandon the need for both.

abandon the credit card bill, the credit scores, the need for credit
borne from lack.

praise the hungry.
abandon those who seek to keep them so. praise the hungry.

praise their empty bodies, empty bellies, empty mouths,
and await the day they will be full.

Eric Torgersen
A BOAT

for Doc, to go

There's a boat, is one old way to picture it:
a river, a boat, and someone at the oars.
And what harm in thinking, even now, of a boat,
a river and a guide to take you over
where the hunting's good and the fishing
and the stories?

With all of us watching, perhaps,
you would step down into the boat,
which would be rocking a little,
and sit, not looking back, till the boat began to go;
we would hear the sound of the oars
growing fainter even when the boat
could no longer be seen.

                    ❋

The daughter I married
sang you off.

What matter
if you had or hadn't read *Lear*?

When I got there, after,
and touched your forehead to feel
your body subsiding
toward the temperature of earth,

I saw the blanket rise
and fall as we'd watched it
rise, fall, rise again for days,

but it was only my breath
lifting and lowering,

away from you, toward you,
away again,
for now.

     ✻

The buck that ran through the field
in this world in bright sunlight was not you;
you were not the three foxes
we saw at the edge of your garden,
not the great buck I fought with in my dream.

We know where your boat is,
we lowered it down with the boats
of the pharaohs and Vikings,
and you are in the boat, and it is not you.

in memoriam E.H.K.

Onna Solomon
MINERAL SONG

It becomes more solid,
more elemental, grows
heavy in my mouth.

All its emptiness—the pauses
for breath—sealed into
hard chambers that can

hold a thing for ages.
And because it becomes a rock,
I treat it like a rock

and walk out into a wild field
to find it a proper home
amid black-eyed Susans and phlox.

This heavy thing
abandoned to the soft mud
of the earth until

finally it breaks, the way
everything breaks eventually,
releasing the breath in it—

my breath in it.
When it happens, maybe
someone will be there

still in that field or, who knows,
in a tidy lawn or at the edge
of a parking lot—

someone will be
there to hear it and wonder
at its recitation.

Elizabeth Porter
HE SAID HE HAD BEEN POCKETING TEA

time for us. From the hospital trays   he palmed
sachets and sugar   packets wrapped them neatly in

cellophane and tucked them in a drawer near clean
Handkerchiefs   I tuck my feet under his legs and

drew nearer to unwrap this gift of time   borrowed
from the future   to smell the malted leaves over the

bet against the odds over the din   of the kettle left
On   high   while empty   and burning

Mae Stier
THE GARDEN

The garden began as a pile of sand, which was not ideal for most of the things I wanted to grow. It was too nutrient deficient, and it would require more work than I was prepared for as a beginning gardener. It was what our family had to work with, and, as I would later find out, the sand worked well for the berry bushes I added during our second season.

We bought the land and the house that sat on it because our options were limited, and this two-and-a-half-acre parcel checked a few boxes: mainly that we could afford the property and also that it offered us a little room to spread out. My partner, Tim, and I had just had our first baby, Daniel, and the small beach cottage I had lived in while I was single no longer suited us. So we searched for anything that fit our price range in northern Michigan, and with limited options settled on a sandy, somewhat-neglected plot with a four-bedroom ranch house. More than enough room for a growing family. We signed the paperwork the day Daniel turned three months old.

I didn't necessarily plan for a garden when we bought the land in early 2020, but somehow I felt beckoned into it, as if the garden itself were always there and I was the one to uncover it. Maybe it was all that time at home with a baby, or perhaps it was the way the pandemic influenced us all to try gardening that spring. Or maybe it was the land itself speaking to me, asking for rejuvenation.

Either way, April 2020 found us almost exclusively at home, so the transformation our yard and the surrounding jack pine forest were begging for began. We started by clearing much of the sand pile that sat where I envisioned our garden. With the help of my parents (their tools, expertise, and baby-wrangling abilities), we built raised beds to offer better control over the garden soil. It was all an experiment, as my gardening knowledge was rather limited.

My mother had kept a garden when we were kids — raspberries, strawberries, and squash — but it was abandoned around the same time as my piano lessons in favor of pursuits that seemed more important. I traded in hours at the piano for basketball practice and calculus homework, and we let the garden slowly grow wild. Nearly two decades after that decision, I now realize that gardening and piano skills would have been much more useful in the long run. I mean, I can still sink a free throw. The calculus, however, has long since left my brain, and the space it used to take up is now filled with more Taylor Swift lyrics than I care to admit.

In college, a stint in an "intentional community house" during college had given me another opportunity to establish a green thumb. But the chaos of living with up to a dozen other college students at any given time, while also hosting various neighborhood events and getting a college degree, made it difficult for me to focus any energy on our little urban garden. My first home in northern Michigan, the little cottage in the village of Empire, had a beautiful garden in the front yard. My landlord's partner, a professional gardener, had planted perennials that needed little tending and gifted me herbs, flowers, and ferns all season long. During my three years living in the cottage, I tried adding additional plants to the yard—hostas, morning glories, hydrangeas—but I hadn't accounted for how much the deer would enjoy them, and none of them survived.

Lack of experience aside, I was determined to grow a garden at our new home, determined that my infant son would be growing alongside tomato and pepper plants that summer. So he and I spent hours each day in the yard with the help of my husband and parents while they were laid off from work because of the pandemic. After they all returned to semi-regular life, it was just Daniel and me digging in the dirt.

Living by the seasons had always been a part of life in Michigan, especially since I had moved to northern Michigan, where we socialize and exercise based on the calendar. Winter affords extra time to visit with friends, and we meet for snowy hikes or fireside drinks to soak up what will seem impossible in the summer months, when our schedules and the region are their busiest. The garden created a new way for me to view the seasons, a new chart for watching my child grow. He was seven months old that May when I began planting, and I probably knew as much about parenting as I did about gardening. But I learned on the go.

In the spring as I worked, he would stay mostly in one place; he was just learning to crawl. By the time we were harvesting vegetables, he was pulling himself up on the plants to pick the peppers himself, taking bites with his four new teeth.

That first spring, we built three raised beds for vegetables, and when I filled those, I dug two additional in-ground beds for flowers and herbs. As my brother's marriage ended two hundred miles away in Grand Rapids that spring, I planted peonies in one of the in-ground beds and cried into the sandy soil as I thought of how our family would change. I sat under the wild cherry tree by the peonies on a phone call with his now ex-wife, Sarah, my best friend of over a decade, and told her about the garden's progress. As summer came, I grieved the years we would never have again, the family vacations that would be forever different, even as the peonies bloomed and the yarrow grew tall. Finally, late in the summer, Sarah came to walk through the garden, to witness the growth in this once barren space.

The following spring, we built a fence around the garden, and I dug more in-ground beds around its edges. Now there was room for peas and cucumbers to trellis up the fence and a perennial bed for planting asparagus and rhubarb. I spent weeks amending the soil, adding compost purchased from a local farm, wood ash from our fire pit, and dirt dug up from decaying tree roots in the woods. I lined the fence on the north side of the garden with the sunflowers, and planted cosmos and dahlias in the new in-ground beds in front of the fence. They began to bloom that August, just before Tim and I got married, and they towered over us all fall.

Tim had bought me a compost system that spring, and I churned it daily throughout the season. We collected our food scraps and carried them out in the evenings. Now a year-and-a-half old, Daniel loved seeing the worms in the bin, would pick them up when he found them in the yard, and carry them to the garden. The compost became my most-loved part of the process. There was something spell-binding about watching waste turn into food for our plants.

One morning, Daniel and I found a dead bird behind the garden; it looked as if it had collided with the fence before falling to the ground. We dug it a hole and buried it where we would transplant raspberries from Grandpa's garden later that fall. As we covered the bird with dirt, I tried to explain to Daniel the circle of life; that part of our purpose comes in death, in returning to the earth. Maybe that was a little over the head of my not-quite-two-year-old, but then again, maybe a little over my head as well.

There was so much death and life flourishing in that garden, these big life moments that swept me off my feet, my face to the earth. I felt, selfishly at times, that the garden was there to teach me, to nurture me. But then so much more of my experience was filled with these little mundane moments where it was clear we were just a piece of the story: Daniel pointing out the bees on the flowers, me painstakingly picking hornworm eggs from the tomato plants. My sweat in the evenings as I went out with a glass of wine, the hose, and my pruning shears to be alone with the plants. All these little gestures, these daily acts that were too small to really keep track of. The compost churning, the plants dying back in the winter; their roots adding nutrients to the soil even under the snow. The gift of black earth in the spring, evidence of the previous few years' tending. It was all slow growth, the kind you don't notice until suddenly it's September, and the tomato plants are as tall as you, the sunflowers stretching to the sky. The same slow growth that I was witnessing in my son — one, two, now three years old. How did it happen so fast?

I knew all along the garden wasn't for me, that caring for this plot of earth was not about the return I would get. Somehow, all that work in the garden was called into existence by the dirt itself, and I was just part of the process. Together I worked with the apple cores and eggshells, the roots from last season's corn, and the dead bird. My energy poured itself back to its origins — the dirt. What we gained in the process was a gift I will always cherish.

We sold the house this summer, and the hardest part was leaving that garden. Every year it had expanded as if on its own, a vision given to me each spring as the snow melted. I always knew it wasn't mine, as the land and waters can never be owned, despite our attempts to lay claim to everything. We pretend that the earth is made up of "developments" and "real estate," even though it will all outlive us, even though the dirt is what we return to. We are just one part of a more remarkable story, gifted the opportunity to get our hands dirty and contribute our slow, steady care. We had just over two years with that piece of earth and then, our time was through.

So we said goodbye to the garden and the peonies I planted the first spring we were there, when my family changed forever. We said goodbye to the raspberry and blueberry patches we had begun. Next spring, someone else will harvest the asparagus and rhubarb, and they will be, for a time, a part of the story for that two and a half acres. May they tend it well. For now, I am learning a new, smaller piece of land, getting to know its contours and animal trails. Following my son's lead as he spends hours moving leaves, shoveling snow, rolling down the hill in the front yard. It is all buried in snow now, and we wait for spring. As the snow melts, I will keep my ears open for the next step, my new role. For direction from the soil for how to best take care.

Betsy Martin
A LITTLE WAVE

how lush!
trees and vines encircle
the house inside
books like lichens
coat the walls

my mother live!
here she takes the compost
in the compost bowl to the far
backyard her dreamy
gray head bowing to the ground

and my father too
in the flesh!
about to make coffee
for the goodbye gathering—
making coffee he says

with a little wave that swells through the decades
and breaks over me

as he places a tray of cups tenderly on the table
I'm there also
prancing about as a thirty-something unicorn
and my brother
with brown hair…

they sell our house—they have to
because the little movie ends
it must

Mary Dean Lee
EAST BEACH

We gather to remember my brother's life.
Nineteen short years, told through letters and postcards,

and the story of my mother, after the crash,
trying to bring him back. I hand out bound copies of *About Bill.*

At the end of East Beach, where Postell Creek winds into marsh,
sandpipers' skinny legs move triple time.

The next wave rolls in. Coquina clams burrow.
Terns scan for bait in the yellow spareness of evening.

A porch door slams, a pelican
lifts with laborious grace.

I lay down in the pale-melon light
as a little protesting voice dies out.

Against the erasing tide, my sand shape changes
from imprint to afterthought to nothing.

Out on the bar, a trail of haze
over the blinking white breakers,

signaling *yes, no, yes, no, yes.*

Eric Torgersen
FOR SUFFERING

Christ Entering Jerusalem on the Back of a Donkey,
Detroit Institute of Art

For suffering, head for the Medieval galleries,
the quiet there, just a few loners ghosting through
while throngs are adoring the Impressionists.

It's not just on crosses, in the laps of sorrowing mothers,
but here in this banged-up Jesus with his bad complexion,
still riding his worm-eaten donkey toward Jerusalem.

If this was ever the son of God it was long ago,
if ever even a man on a donkey, or anything more
after centuries than the wood, exhausted, the wood itself
wanting it over, yearning toward Jerusalem to die.

LC Gutierrez
WHEN YOU, AS A YOUNGER MAN, WATCHED ME UNDER WATER

Know there are pieces of me where you pointed
but didn't take my hand. There was happiness

in childhood, I'm sure, though I recall
the rest, where I grew up in shreds

alone. And really, who can blame
memory, which has its chosen process?

Your missing touch was my mirror
for your own bent craving:

how you yourself were raised in strained
and choked affections. And then

how you drank your coffee black.
The warm scent of it won't come

to mind, but oh, that mug you smashed
in rage, sparing me your fists,

father, keeping me small and sad
and wishing I could shatter and shard

to show you I was worthy, too,
of rended sacrifice. Then my comfort taken

in breaking my self, my chest
a daggered field. Now, untangled

my infant voice, the only swaddling sound
I carry bound for the both of us,

my lips now bless your forehead. Pull you close
as though you were my child.

Jack Ridl
JUST OUTSIDE THE WINDOW

There's a robin doing its start and
stop walk across the lawn, and I
just finished talking on the phone

to my old friend who lives in assisted
living. He's two years older, and I am
here writing this and wondering why.

The moon will be here any minute, robin.
You better get home. The eggs will
soon be in your nest. Every year I find

a broken, shagged-edged light blue.
My friend tells me, "I'm fine and useless."
I wish he hadn't worked so hard every

waking day and hadn't spent remembering
the Sabbath to keep it holy, reading his
Bible every evening. The moon is higher now.

I think about happiness. I hope the robin is home.
I used to get weekly letters from home. Now
each morning I watch for the robin, hoping.

Maybe tomorrow I'll go downtown, walk
into some stores and say, "Thanks. Just looking."

CONTRIBUTOR BIOS

*CONNOR BEEMAN (he/they) is a queer Midwest poet who focuses on queerness, place, nature, and history. They are the winner of the 2022 Ritzenhein Emerging Poet Award and the author of concrete, rust, marrow (Finishing Line Press, 2023). Other recent publications include *The Fourth River* and *Ghost City Review*.

*Originally from Los Angeles, JUDY Y. CHU has lived in Traverse City for almost 25 years now, where she, her husband, and their daughter are herded by their Shetland sheepdog. An English faculty member at Northwestern Michigan College, she teaches freshman composition.

JOHN DAVIS is the author of *Gigs* (Sol Books) and a chapbook, The Reservist. His work appears in *DMQ Review, One, Poetry Northwest, Sycamore Review* and Terrain.org. After forty years of teaching high school, he has retired and moonlights in a local blues band. He adores peaches.

MATT DENNISON is the author of *Kind Surgery*, from Urtica Press (Fr.) and *Waiting for Better*, from Main Street Rag Press. His work has appeared in *Verse Daily, Rattle, Bayou Magazine, Redivider and Cider Press Review*, among others. He has also made short films with Marie Craven and Jutta Pryor.

DEAN ENGLE is a writer and college instructor from the Bay Area. His work has appeared in *Santa Ana River Review, Great Lakes Review, Brushfire, Toyon, ideaFest, New Plains Review, Clackamas Literary Review*, and *On the Run*. In his spare time, he likes making soup and overwatering house plants.

LC GUTIERREZ is a product of many places in the South and the Caribbean. He now writes, teaches and plays trombone in Madrid, Spain. His work is recently published in *Autofocus, Notre Dame Review, Sweet, Hobart, Across the Margin* and other wonderful journals.

KEN HINES has been an advertising writer and college English teacher, two jobs that require getting through to people who aren't always interested in what you have to say. His poems appear in *AIOTB, Psaltery & Lyre, Burningwood Journal* and other magazines. He lives in Virginia with his wife, Fran.

MAD HOWARD is a Creative Writing teacher in Phoenix, Arizona. She graduated from Northern Arizona University with a BA in English and graduated from Albertus Magnus College with an MFA in Creative Writing. When not writing, she is probably teaching her rabbit a new trick. This is the first time she has been published.

STEPHANIE KEEP is a writer living in Montana. Her poetry practice has come as a welcome surprise borne of long walks, first along the streets of San Francisco and now on the trails of her native Mountain West. In every creative venture, she's looking for interesting, not perfect.

DIVYASRI KRISHNAN is a writer from Massachusetts. Her work has been published in *DIAGRAM, Muzzle Magazine, Annulet,* and elsewhere. She has further been recognized by the Best of the Net, Kenyon Review Writers Workshops, Periplus Collective, Pittsburgh Humanities Festival, and Palette Poetry.

BEE LB is an array of letters, bound to impulse; a writer creating delicate connections. they have called any number of places home; currently, a single yellow wall in Michigan. they have been published in *FOLIO, Roanoke Review, and Landfill,* among others. they are a poetry reader for *Capsule Stories.*

JENNA LE (jennalewriting.com) is author of three full-length collections, *Six Rivers* (NYQ Books, 2011); *A History of the Cetacean American Diaspora* (Indolent Books, 2017), an Elgin Awards Second Place winner; and *Manatee Lagoon* (Acre Books, 2022). A daughter of Vietnamese refugees, she works as a physician in New York City.

MARY DEAN LEE's poetry has appeared or is forthcoming in *Best Canadian Poetry 2021, Burningword, Ploughshares, I-70 Review, LEON Literary Review* and elsewhere. Raised in Milledgeville, Georgia, she studied theatre and literature at Duke and Eckerd College, received her PhD in organizational behavior at Yale. She lives in Montreal, Canada.

*ELLEN LORD is a Michigan native and behavioral health therapist. Her writing has appeared in *Dunes Review, Walloon Writers Review, U.P. Reader, Haiku Society of America, R.k.v.r.y Quarterly Literary Journal, Peninsula Poets* anthologies and elsewhere. She is a member of Michigan Writers and the Upper Peninsula Publishers & Authors Association.

MICHAEL MARK is the author of *Visiting Her in Queens is More Enlightening than a Month in a Monastery in Tibet* which won the 2022 Rattle Chapbook Prize. His poems appear or are forthcoming in *Copper Nickel, Ploughshares, Poetry Northwest, Sixth Finch, The Southern Review, The Sun, 32 Poems.* Michaeljmark.com

BETSY MARTIN is the author of the poetry chapbook, *Whale's Eye* (Presa Press, 2019). Her poetry has appeared in *The Briar Cliff Review, California Quarterly, The Louisville Review, The MacGuffin,* and The *Midwest Quarterly,* among other journals. She long studied Russian language and is also a visual artist. Betsymartinpoet.com

*PAUL MAXBAUER, a retired history teacher, lives in Traverse City, Michigan. He now spends his time writing poems and short stories. His work has appeared in the Poets Night Out chapbook by the Traverse Area District Library, *Walloon Writers Review,* and *Dunes Review.*

*SEAN MCFADDEN received his B.A. in English from the University of Michigan, then all bets were off. He's currently editing his backwards-moving novel of short stories, *Peeling the Onion*. Recent work is in *Drunk Monkeys* and *The Write Launch*, and is forthcoming at *After Happy Hour Review* and *The Lakeshore Review*.

ZACKARY MEDLIN is an award-winning poet whose work has appeared in journals such as *Colorado Review, The Cincinnati Review,* and *Mid-American Review*. He earned his M.F.A from the University of Alaska Fairbanks and his Ph.D. from the University of Utah. He lives in Colorado, where he teaches at Fort Lewis College.

KURT OLSSON's poems have appeared in a wide variety of publications, including *Poetry, The Threepenny Review, and Southern Review*. He's published two poetry collections, *Burning Down Disneyland* (Gunpowder Press) and *What Kills What Kills Us* (Silverfish Review Press). A third collection, *The Unnumbered Anniversaries*, is due out in 2024.

RENÉ OSTBERG is a freelance writer from Illinois. Her work has appeared in *Sojourners, National Catholic Reporter*, the *Brevity* blog, *Hobart*, and many other places. She is currently pursuing a degree in library science at Dominican University. Her website is reneostberg.com.

*DIANE PAYNE's most recent publications include *Cutleaf Journal, Your Impossible Voice, Miracle Monacle, Hairstreak Butterfly, Table Feast Literary Magazine, Invisible City, Miramichi Flash Best of Microfiction2022, Spry Literary Magazine, Persimmon, Another Chicago Magazine, Whale Road Review, Fourth River, Tiny Spoon,* and *Bending Genres*. More can be found here: dianepayne.wordpress.com

JANUARY PEARSON's work has appeared or is forthcoming in *Los Angeles Review, Poetry South, Tahoma Literary Review, 2River, Rust + Moth, Notre Dame Review,* and other publications. She was named a finalist by the editors of The Best of the Net 2020 Anthology.

*JACK RIDL's *All at Once* will be published by CavanKerry Press in 2024. Poet, editor, and educator, he is the author of several award-winning poetry collections and anthologies. He won awards from the Society of Midland Authors, the NYC Center for the Book, and the Institute for International Sports. He was Carnegie Foundation's Michigan Professor of the Year. www.ridl.com

As a mathematical Babtist, RADOSLAV ROCHALLYI builds poetry in mathematical terms. He believes that math is a matter between God and the individual.

ELLEN WHITE ROOK is a poet, writer, and contemplative arts teacher living in upstate New York and Maine. Author of the poetry collection *Suspended* (Cathexis Northwest Press, 2023), she leads workshops and retreats that merge meditation, mindful movement, and writing. Read more of her work at ellenwhiterook.com.

RICHARD RUBIN is a retired librarian and library educator who has been writing poetry for personal satisfaction for many years. Recently, he decided to try and publish some of his current work and he has been fortunate to have poems accepted in *Great Lakes Review, Green Silk Review, Willows Wept Review, Kakalak* and others.

*LINDA K. SIENKIEWICZ's work has appeared in numerous literary journals and anthologies. She has five Finalist Awards for her novel, *In the Context of Love*, and a poetry chapbook award from Heartlands. Her fifth poetry chapbook is titled *Sleepwalker*. She holds an MFA from the University of Southern Maine. LindaKSienkiewicz.com [Editor's note: Sienkiewicz's poems in this issue were originally published in *Sleepwalker* by Finishing Line Press.]

*ONNA SOLOMON's poems have appeared in *Beloit Poetry Journal, Cimarron Review, Denver Quarterly, 32 Poems*, and *Crab Creek Review,* among others. Her poem "Autism Suite" was awarded *Beloit Poetry Journal*'s Chad Walsh Poetry Prize. She lives in Ann Arbor, MI.

*PHILLIP STERLING's most recent collection of poetry, *Local Congregation: Poems Uncollected 1985-2015*, is scheduled for publication by Main Street Rag in Fall 2023. His collection of essays and memoir, *Lessons in Geography: The Education of a Michigan Poet*, will be released in 2024.

ANDREW STEVENS is a Seattle writer, published in *The Journal of Compressed Creative Arts, The Bookends Review,* and *The Gold Man Review*. He is working on additional stories and poems and larger writing projects that maybe someday he will finish.

*MAE STIER is a writer and photographer living in northern Michigan. She writes about life near Lake Michigan and has a self-published collection of poetry and essays entitled *Lake Letters*, available on her website, lakeletters.com. She lives with her husband and two small children in Empire.

PABLO PIÑERO STILLMANN's work has appeared in, among other journals, *Ninth Letter, Bennington Review, Mississippi Review*, and *Blackbird*. His story collection, *Our Brains and the Brains of Miniature Sharks,* was released in 2020 from Moon City Press.

RANA TAHIR is a poet and author living in Portland, OR. She earned her MFA from Pacific University. She is a Kundiman Fellow and member of RAWI. www.rana-tahir.com

MATT THOMAS is a smallholder farmer and occasional community college teacher. His work has appeared recently in *River Heron Review, Killing the Buddha,* and *Cleaver Magazine*. He lives with his partner in the Blue Ridge Mountains of Virginia.

*RUSSELL THORBURN is a playwright and author of *Somewhere We'll Leave the World*. An NEA Fellow and first poet laureate of Michigan's Upper Peninsula, he lives in Marquette with his wife. His next book, *Let It Be Told in a Single Breath*, is forthcoming in 2024.

*ERIC TORGERSEN taught creative writing at Central Michigan University for 38 years. His most recent book is *In Which We See Our Selves: American Ghazals*, Mayapple Press. He is also the author of *Dear Friend: Rainer Maria Rilke and Paula Modersohn-Becker*, Northwestern University Press.

*ANN WILLEY is an artist living in Michigan. She often works in the narrative art tradition, inspired by her love of nature, folktales and stories. She began her career as a graphic artist and illustrator and later switched her focus primarily to painting and fiber art. See more at Annwilley.com

PATRICIA AYA WILLIAMS is a Red Wheelbarrow Poetry Prize recipient and Steve Kowit Poetry Prize finalist. Her work has appeared in *Santa Clara Review*, *The Good Life Review*, *San Diego Poetry Annual*, *Writers Resist*, and *Origami Poems Project*. In 2022, her poem "Ichiban" was nominated for a Pushcart Prize.

READER BIOS

*ASHWINI BHASI is a bioinformatician from Kerala, India who is exploring the somatics of shame, trauma, and chronic pain through poetry and visual art. Her chapbook, *Musth*, was winner of the 2020 CutBank chapbook contest. Her work can be found in *Michigan Quarterly Review*, *RHINO*, *Frontier Poetry*, *The Offing* and elsewhere.

*SHEENA M. CAREY, M.A., is internship director and lecturer for the Diederich College of Communication at Marquette University, and a consultant in intercultural and DEI work. She has collaborated with Coyaba Dance Theater in Washington, DC. and the Ko-Thi Dance Company in Milwaukee, WI. She writes and performs spoken word poetry.

*KELLI FITZPATRICK is an author, editor, and teacher from Michigan. Her fiction has been published by Simon and Schuster, *Flash Fiction Online*, *Crazy 8 Press*, and others. She has edited for Modiphius Entertainment, the *Journal of Popular Culture*, and San Jose State University. Website: KelliFitzpatrick.com

*CHRIS GIROUX received his doctorate from Wayne State University and is a professor of English at Saginaw Valley State University, where he has served as faculty advisor for the school's literary magazine and co-founded the community arts journal *Still Life*. His second chapbook, *Sheltered in Place*, was released in 2022.

*ANNE-MARIE OOMEN's memoir, *As Long As I Know You: The Mom Book* won AWP's Sue William Silverman Nonfiction Award. She wrote *Lake Michigan Mermaid* with Linda Nemec Foster (Michigan Notable Book), *Love, Sex and 4-H* (Next Generation Indie Award/Memoir), and others. Her new book, *The Long Fields*, launches August 2023.

*JOHN MAUK has published a range of stories and nonfiction works, including his first full collection, *Field Notes for the Earthbound*. His second, *Where All Things Flatten,* will be available in 2024. John also hosts Prose from the Underground, a YouTube video series for working writers. For more information, see johnmauk.com.

*TERESA SCOLLON's recent publications include the poetry collection *Trees and Other Creatures* (Alice Greene) and an essay in *Elemental*, an anthology of Michigan essayists (Wayne State University Press). A National Endowment for the Arts fellow, she teaches the Writers Studio program at North Ed Career Tech in Traverse City.

*JENNIFER YEATTS' literary life has included MA and MFA degrees in poetry, teaching writing in various forms, and editorial roles at *Passages North* and *Fugue*. Magically, she has found a professional livelihood in the world of specialty coffee.

*denotes Michigan native or resident

SUBMISSION GUIDELINES

Dunes Review welcomes work from writers at all stages of their careers living anywhere in the world, though we particularly love featuring those with ties to Michigan and the Midwest. We are open to all styles and aesthetics, but please read the following carefully to dive a little deeper into what we're looking for.

Ultimately, we're looking for work that draws us in from the very first line: with image, with sound, with sense, with lack of sense. We're looking for writing that makes us *feel* and bowls us over, lifts us up, and takes us places we've never been to show us ordinary things in ways we've never seen them. We're looking for poems and stories and essays that teach us how to read them and pull us back to their beginnings as soon as we've read their final lines. We're looking for things we can't wait to read again, things we can't wait to share with the nearest person who will listen. Send us your best work. We'll give it our best attention.

Submissions are accepted only via our Submittable platform: www.dunesreview.submittable.com. We do not consider work sent through postal mail or email. Any submissions sent through email will not be read or responded to. Please see further guidelines posted on our site. We look forward to reading your work!

Call for Patrons

Dunes Review is a not-for-profit endeavor to promote creative work within the Northern Michigan writing community and beyond.

The cost of publication can be underwritten in part by individual contributions. We invite you to support the publication of the next issue with a donation of $50.

Send your check payable
to **Michigan Writers** to:

Michigan Writers
P.O. Box 2355
Traverse City, MI 49685

Thank you in advance for your support!

110

Printed in the USA
CPSIA information can be obtained
at www.ICGtesting.com
BVHW041138300723
667919BV00003B/19